I think it's time I had a haircut!

(and a bath)

THE AMAZING ADVENTURES OF CHARLIE SMALL (400)

Notebook 8

Pong!

FOREST OF SKULLS

Peep!

RED FOX

CHARLIE SMALL: FOREST OF SKULLS
A RED FOX BOOK 978 1 782 95321 0

First published in Great Britain by David Fickling Books,
(when an imprint of Random House Children's Publishers UK
A Random House Group Company)

This Red Fox edition published 2014

3 5 7 9 10 8 6 4

**Penguin Random House is committed to a sustainable future for
our business, our readers and our planet. This book is made from
Forest Stewardship Council® certified paper.**

MIX
Paper from
responsible sources
FSC® C018179
FSC
www.fsc.org

Set in 15/17pt Garamond MT

Red Fox Books are published by Random House Children's Publishers UK,
61–63 Uxbridge Road, London W5 5SA

www.**randomhousechildrens**.co.uk
www.**totallyrandombooks**.co.uk
www.**randomhouse**.co.uk

Addresses for companies within The Random House Group Limited can be found at:
www.**randomhouse**.co.uk/offices.htm

THE RANDOM HOUSE GROUP Limited Reg. No. 954009

A CIP catalogue record for this book is available from the British Library.

Printed and bound in Great Britain by Clays Ltd, St Ives plc

NAME: Charlie Small

ADDRESS: The Forest of Skulls

AGE: I'm an eight-year-old boy who's lived for 400 years!

MOBILE: 07713 1238

SCHOOL: I haven't been to school for centuries!

THINGS I LIKE: Jakeman and Philly; the bull whale; Barcus and Knee-high; my dad!

THINGS I HATE: Joseph Craik (my arch enemy); Captain Cut-throat and Mildew Jones; smelly, hairy rats and wily weasels

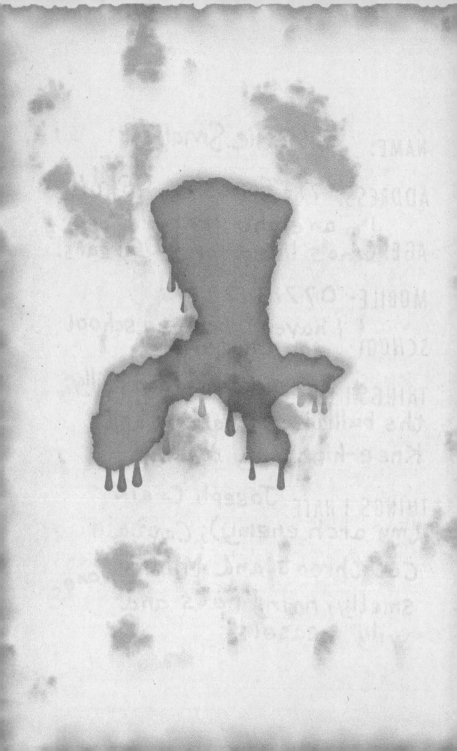

If you find this book, <u>PLEASE</u> look after it. This is the only true account of my remarkable adventures.

My name is Charlie Small and I am at least four hundred years old. But in all those long years I have never grown up. Something happened when I was eight, something I can't begin to understand. I went on a journey... and I'm still trying to find my way home. Now, although I've ridden across oceans on the back of a big bull whale, been nearly skewered by loathsome giant rats and lived in the leafy roof of a forest, I still look like any eight-year-old boy you might pass in the street.

I've tackled a rabid badger in mortal combat and driven a rampaging armoured armadillo. You might think this sounds fantastic, you could think it's a lie, but you would be wrong. Because EVERYTHING <u>IN THIS BOOK IS TRUE.</u> Believe this single fact and you can share the most incredible journey ever experienced!

<u>Charlie Small</u>

'Welcome 'ome,' cried Lizzie Hall

Prisoner Of The Perfumed Pirates - Again!

'Weigh anchor and hoist the mainsail!' bellowed Captain Cut-throat as we stepped aboard her galleon. The night was dark, but a score of lanterns lit the deck with a hazy, golden light.

Half a dozen lady pirates ran over to the capstan and began to heave against the bars, their ghastly tattoos twitching as the muscles of their sinewy arms took the strain of the big, heavy anchor.

'Welcome 'ome, Charlie Small,' cried Lizzie Hall.

'Yeah! There'll be no escapin' this time, you desertin' dog!' sneered Sabre Sue, grunting as the wheel started to turn and the heavy anchor's chain coiled into the ship.

'Don't you worry yourselves,' growled the captain, clamping her large fist around my wrist. 'This little worm ain't going nowhere. Now, get on with your jobs, you putrid pile of pilchard guts!'

With the anchor lifted from the ocean floor, a large, stained and torn sail was hoisted up the main mast. The galleon turned on a swell of water, the sail filled with air and we headed out into the open seas.

'Right, me hearties,' bellowed the captain as we sliced through the waves with silver bubbles streaming along the bows, 'let's go a-piratin'!'

I gave a huge sigh. Darn it and double drat! Why oh why did this have to happen *now*?

Snatched!

Just an hour earlier, I'd been safely tucked up in bed inside Jakeman's factory, wondering how my miraculous inventor friend was going to get me back home. (I've been away for four hundred years – and Mum is still expecting me back in time for tea!)

'Don't worry your head about that, dear boy,' Jakeman had beamed. 'I've been working on various inventions ever since I promised to get you home. Some haven't quite worked out; some have been downright disasters! But now I think I've got it – I shoot you from a special cannon straight through my Atom-Annihilating Archway, which will take you right back to the world you came from.'

'Fire me from a cannon?' I said, feeling a bit concerned. 'Are you sure this invention's safe?'

'Well, one can never be one hundred per cent sure in this game, Charlie. All I know is that I fired a woodlouse through the arch and it disappeared and never came back. If my calculations were correct, it should have gone to your world.'

'What if your calculations *weren't* correct?' I stammered. 'What if the woodlouse ended up on some distant star, populated by bug-eyed monstrous Martians? That could be me!'

'Now, don't worry so much. I'm sure that won't happen,' said Jakeman. 'You go and get a good night's sleep and I'll show you the Jakeman Archway to Anywhere in the morning.'

A bug-eyed Martian

(See my journal The Mummy's Tomb!)

I was pretty tired, having ridden the waves all day in a super-speedy hover-sub and then fought Tristam Twitch's two moronic minders, so I climbed the stairs to the top of the warehouse and crawled into the oil-stained bed that Jakeman had made up for me.

I hadn't been in bed more than an hour when I heard a loud noise. I'd been busy writing up my journal and wondering if I really would get home in the morning, or be zapped to yet another unknown world, when a hoarse cry rang out from along the corridor.

'Where are you, Charlie Small?'

Oh no! I recognize that voice, I thought. It's that fearsome lady pirate, Captain Cut-throat! What on earth is she doing here?

'Come on, there's no use hidin' lad, where are you?' she bellowed.

Oh yikes! I desperately reached for my cutlass as the door to my room burst open with a mighty *crash* . . . and there was Cut-throat herself, looking twice as ugly and three times as mean as the last time I'd seen her. Her broad, pug-nosed face broke into a grin that exposed a row of blackened teeth.

'Stay right where you are, you snivellin' slime-nosed slug,' she bawled. 'Touch that cutlass and I'll open your gizzard and see what you had for dinner!'

'Clear off, Cut-throat,' I said, although I didn't feel half as brave as I was trying to sound. 'What do you want, anyway?'

'You, ya little rapscallion,' she said in a low growl. 'It's about time you returned to your pirating duties!'

'You've got to be kidding!' I said. 'There's no way I'm going to pilfer and pillage for you again.'

Marching across the room, Cut-throat grabbed my cutlass and snapped it over her knee, and then seized me by the scruff of the neck.

'Less of your backchat, lad,' she crowed. 'Just remember who you're talkin' to. Now, get yourself ready and meet me downstairs in five minutes. We've got your pals nicely trussed up, so don't try any funny business.'

With that, the pirate slammed the door closed and I heard her heavy boots clumping down the passage.

A Pirate Once More!

I got dressed in a panic, pulling on my tatty jeans and holey top. The last thing I wanted to do was go pirating again but I thought I'd better be prepared for the worst, so packed everything I might need in my trusty explorer's rucksack. Nervously, I made my way downstairs, past floors of dilapidated machinery and along corridors lined with old chests spilling large diagrams of ingenious inventions all over the floor.

At the bottom of the staircase, I entered the main workshop and saw Captain Cut-throat over by one of the lathes on the far side. With her was Rawcliffe Annie, another of the dreaded Perfumed Pirate gang. She was as tough as hickory, with a nose like a hatchet that she used to crack open coconuts.

'Why, here's my old pal Black-hearted Charlie,' she cried. 'How's the most wanted pirate on the high seas? Oh, didn't you know your best friend was wanted on two continents?' she added, looking down at her feet. As I turned into the walkway I saw Philly and Jakeman, tied up at her feet in a tangle of rope and knots. They both

had gags around their
mouths.

'Mmm, mmm,
mmm!' mumbled
Philly, angrily frowning
at the smirking pirate.

'Oh, I know. It's
terrible isn't it?'
continued Annie.
'He's not a very suitable
companion for a nice young
lady like you. But no need to worry
– you won't have to put up with him any more.
He's comin' with us.'

'No, sorry, I've made up my mind,' I said,
crossing my arms defiantly. 'I'm not going
anywhere with you.'

'Oh yes you are, Charlie,' replied Rawcliffe
Annie, thrusting her long chin forward.

'Not!'

'Yes, you bloomin' are!' yelled Cut-throat,
grabbing me viciously around the wrist and
yanking me to her side. 'I said I didn't want any
trouble from you, you squirt. Or do you want
me to slice off the top of your pals' skulls, like
a couple of boiled eggs?' And with that Captain

Cut-throat span her cutlass around her head until it was just a blur, the blade singing through the air.

'No!' I cried. 'Don't do that!' I knew Captain Cut-throat could be the world's blood-thirstiest pirate if something got in her way. 'I'll come, just let them be. What do you want me for anyway?'

'Because you're a fully-fledged pirate, boy; once you've signed up to the pirate code, you're a pirate *forever*; no one escapes from the sisterhood, not even a scrawny, no-good boy like you. And that reminds me; you can give me that rucksack of yours,' demanded Cut-throat.

'No way!' I cried. 'You're not having my explorer's kit. I need that to help me get home.'

'Don't you understand, you useless bag o' bones, *you ain't ever goin' home*?' the captain thundered, slamming a fist down onto the workbench and making a tall brass microscope topple over. 'Now, give me that bag before I do somethin' appallingly piratical!'

I reluctantly slipped my precious rucksack from my shoulders and handed it over. Captain Cut-throat laid it on the bench and, grabbing the microscope, brought it smashing down onto the buttons that controlled the jet-thrusters on the bottom. The buttons fizzed and sparked as the plastic casing shattered, and a small puff of smoke floated into the air.

'No!' I cried, as Cut-throat handed me back the ruined bag. 'How did you know about that?'

'Oh, there's not much gets past me, you pusillanimous pustule. I've heard all about your miraculous jet-powered rucksack. Now you won't be able to fly away when the fancy takes you!'

Dash, blow and double darn it! Mamuk the reindeer herder had given me that flying rucksack for rescuing him from the Barbarous Brigands. Now it was just a normal bag again.

'Mmm, mmm, mmm,' mumbled Philly, rocking to and fro and straining against her bonds. 'Mmm, mmm, *mmm*!'

'Are you trying to say something?' asked Cut-throat, removing Philly's gag.

'Take me instead of Charlie,' she gasped. 'Let him go home to his mum and dad.'

'No, Philly!' I cried. I was amazed at what a loyal friend she was. She was prepared to give up her freedom in order to save me! 'I could never ask you to do that.'

(See my Journal Frostbite Pass)

'Quiet!' snapped Captain Cut-throat. 'It's got nothin' to do with either of you. Now, let me think a bit . . .' She rubbed her ruddy chin with the palm of a large hand. 'No! I'll take Charlie,' she said. 'Me an' him 'ave got unfinished business, 'aven't we lad?'

I gulped and nodded my head. 'I suppose so,' I said. 'But at least untie my friends before we go.'

'Ha! I wasn't born yesterday, Charlie,' scoffed Cut-throat. 'You don't think I'm gonna free 'em so they can follow us in that new-fangled crab boat of theirs, do you?' She saw my look of surprise and chuckled. 'Oh yes, I know all about the Crustacean Hover-sub as well! I have spies everywhere.'

'At least let me give Charlie a keepsake to take with him,' said Philly.

'A keepsake? What sort of keepsake?' asked Cut-throat suspiciously.

'Just a little trinket box, to remember me by. It's on that bench, there,' said my friend. I was touched that Philly wanted to give me a present.

Cut-throat picked up a small box from the table. It was very plain with just a simple forget-me-not painted on the lid. The pirate captain flipped it open – it was empty inside. 'It's not worth nothin',' she scoffed. 'What do you want to give him this for? Is he your lovey-dovey boyfriend or something?'

This is a sketch of the little box Philly gave to me

Why did she want me to have it, I wonder?

'It's just a memento,' sighed Philly. 'Haven't you ever given anyone a present?'

'No!' said the captain. Then snapping the lid shut she gave it to me. I turned it over in my hand. It was a thoroughly unremarkable box and I wondered why Philly wanted me to have it.

'Thanks, Philly,' I said, and put it into my pocket.

'Right, come on, Charlie, we've got to go,' said Captain Cut-throat. Taking a long chain from under her coat, she grabbed my arm and with a quick movement flicked a heavy manacle around my wrist. The other end was fixed to her belt. 'Just in case you're thinkin' of scarperin' again,' she said. 'And remember what I said. No funny business, or this time I'll send you down to shake hands with Davy Jones himself.'

'Bye Jakeman. Bye Philly,' I called sadly over
my shoulder as I was dragged out through the
factory doors on my lead. The night was warm
and the air filled with the scent of heather and
the salty smell of the sea.

'Cheer up, Charlie,'
chuckled Rawcliffe
Annie. 'You're a
pirate again!'

Oh brilliant, I
thought. That's just
what I need!

Rawcliffe
Annie

The Ghastly Galleon

As the moon came out from behind a bank
of black clouds, Cut-throat and Annie led me
across the windswept, grassy cliff-tops. We
pushed into a tangle of gorse bushes near
to the cliff-edge and, just as I thought I
was going to be marched right out
into thin air, we climbed into
a hole at our feet which
was hidden by long

tufts of coarse grass. We emerged out on a narrow path that clung precariously to the cliff-face.

In single file we tramped down the path, loosening showers of stones that tumbled to the rocks below. The treacherous track weaved back and forth down the cliff and I hugged the rock-face like a limpet, expecting the path to crumble beneath my feet at any minute. Eventually, we stepped onto a small patch of shingle at the base.

We were hidden in dense black shadows that cast ghastly shapes across the pebbled beach. The sea crashed all around us, and the faint ghostly shapes of seagulls circled overhead, screaming down at us with shrill cries. I was soaked in seconds by huge frothing waves as my captors hauled me onto an outcrop of rough boulders and pushed me across the top to where a dinghy was waiting, tied to a rusty ring in the rock.

'In you get,' said the captain and, still attached to the bullying pirate, I jumped down into the boat. Soon Annie was heaving on the oars and we moved dangerously along a jagged spit of rocks. As we reached the end and rowed out into open sea, I saw the pirates' galleon some hundred metres from the shore. I gasped in shock, for I had been expecting to see our old ship the *Betty Mae* – but now I remembered I'd discovered her rotted and abandoned hulk in Subterranea. What I did see made my eyes bulge in disbelief!

The Perfumed Pirates' new galleon was the most incredible heap of floating flotsam I had ever seen. It looked like a rubbish tip with sails. The hull was made entirely of metal; scraps of tin, corrugated iron, discarded panels, all bolted, riveted and welded together in the most haphazard fashion. In places the metal shone in the moonlight, elsewhere it was rusty and storm-blackened. It looked half comical and half very, very scary!

'What do ye think of our new home, Charlie?' asked the captain proudly. 'We made her ourselves.'

'Fancy,' I said.

'We had to abandon the old *Betty Mae* after a misunderstanding with the Pangaean Navy. So we built a new one made of metal; she's an unsinkable floating fortress and the most heavily armed galleon on the high seas. Nothing can stop us!'

(see my journal The Underworld)

As we got closer, I saw what Cut-throat meant. Weapons were mounted in every available space. Scores of cannon poked out from gun ports. More were positioned on the deck. Blunderbusses, harpoons, and hunting rifles were bolted to the masts and rails. It was bristling with weaponry! The closer we got to the black, rusting hulk, the scarier it looked.

'We call her the *Judgement Day*, for that's what she surely is to anyone that gets in our way,' grinned the captain.

I gulped. Although the ship looked like a pile of junk, it was terrifying!

'Ahoy there!' yelled Captain Cut-throat. 'We're comin' aboard!'

Immediately a rope ladder was thrown over the side and we clambered up and stepped onto the deck. With a squeaking of pulleys the dinghy was hauled up after us, and for the first time in years I was stranded aboard a pirate ship. Oh, yikes!

Now we have weighed anchor and are heading across the wide, swelling ocean. I've been shown to my cabin – a tiny metal room on the lower deck with one jagged porthole cut into the side.

The room is very bare, with just a tin trunk for storage and a moth-eaten hammock strung between two hooks on the walls. A weak light is flickering from a candleholder by the door, throwing the corners of the rusty room into shifting, dark shadows. Oh, lovely, home sweet home! At least it's not as smelly as the old *Betty Mae*.

I'm just bringing my journal up to date – then I'm going to get some sleep. A blowzy buccaneer is standing guard outside my door, so there's no chance of sneaking away tonight. In the morning though, I'll have to start planning an escape. I don't want to spend any longer with these pernicious pirates than I have to!

I'll write more when I can . . .

Mildew Jones

Oh, blimey! You'll *never* guess where I am now. I'm sitting on the back of . . . no! I'd better tell everything in the right order . . .

Early the next morning, a rap on the door woke me from a troubled sleep. I had tossed and turned all night, unable to get comfy in my rough, knotty hammock and kept awake by the booming of the sea against the galleon's metal sides. Every time I nodded off, the noise of pirates clanking about the decks or the squeaks and scratching of red-eyed rats under my string bed woke me up.

'What do you want?' I mumbled sleepily.

The door opened with a creak, and a pirate I'd never seen before stepped into the cabin. She was a tall, whip-thin wizened old crone with greasy hair that hung down to her shoulders in rat-tails. She had a filthy, slimy apron on and a runny nose, which she wiped in great streaks across her sleeve. Clamped between her brown teeth was a stinky old cigar that dropped a continuous trail of ash on the floor.

'Ged up. Cabtain wants yer,' she mumbled through her thick cold.

'Who are you?' I asked. 'You're not one of the Perfumed Pirates!'

'Ab so,' she said, spitting bits of tobacco on the floor. 'I'b Bildew Jones the ship's new cook, if it's any business of yours.'

The *cook*? I thought. All of a sudden I wasn't looking forward to my breakfast! Here is a drawing of the ghastly gastronome:

Mildew Jones

'Cub on, shake a leg, boy, or you'll end ub sizzlin' in me fryin' ban!'

I rolled out of my hammock, picked up my rucksack and followed the spindly pirate out of my room and down the passage.

'Time to find out what the cabtain's got in store for ya,' said Mildew, spitting on the floor again. 'Whateber it is, you can be sure it won't be very bleasant. Hee, hee!'

The pirates were busy about their chores and hardly looked up as we crossed the clanking deck to the captain's cabin. Mildew rapped on the door.

'Cabin boy to see you, Cabtain,' she bellowed, but before the captain could reply, a hoarse cry came from up in the crow's nest.

'Oh, goody, goody yum-yum,' smiled Mildew.

'There what blows?' I asked.

'*Oof!*' The captain's door crashed open, knocking me to the ground.

'Get up, you lazy good-for-nuthin',' yelled Cut-throat, stepping over me and charging onto the deck. She had an excited and hungry look on her face. 'This ain't time for restin'. We're gonna need every hand we can get.'

The Leviathan

Feeling slightly dazed, I climbed up to the poop deck after the captain. The rest of the crew were leaning over the side of the ship, pointing and chattering excitedly.

'Man the harpoons,' bellowed Captain Cutthroat, and immediately some of the pirates broke away and took up position behind the three large harpoon guns on board. There was one at the front and one on each side of the *Judgement Day*, and they were armed with the most horrendous, deadly missiles; thick, vicious-looking barbed spears.

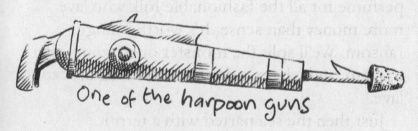

One of the harpoon guns

'What's happening?' I asked, feeling confused. I hadn't been able to see anything beyond the crowd of pirates.

'Dinner, that's what's habbenin'',' guffawed the cook, licking her lips, and the rest of the crew cheered. 'Make way, you lubbers – let the dog see the rabbit.' The crew parted and I looked out to sea. It was empty!

'But there's nothing there,' I said.

'It's a whale, you nit,' scoffed Mildew. 'About a mile out. It's just dived under de water, but it'll come ub again, don't you worry. That means lovely whale steaks to eat, whale oil to sell and, if we're lucky, a nice lump of ambergris to auction off to the highest bidder!'

'What's ambergris?' I asked.

'Don't you know nothin'?' bawled Captain Cut-throat. 'It's a strange, waxy stuff only found inside a whale's gut. They use it to make perfume for all the fashionable folk who 'ave more money than sense. It's worth a king's ransom. We'll split the monster open from stern to stem, and what we don't use the seagulls can 'ave.'

Just then the sea parted with a terrific whooshing noise and the whale surfaced, now only about five hundred metres from our boat.

'Wow! It's a monster!' gasped Mildew. 'A bloomin' great bull whale.'

'He's magnificent,' I said as the animal shot a spout of water from his blowhole. His massive blunt head was as big as the cab of a truck and was covered in scars and bumps and warts. The whale's back hunched in a high arc to a small, bumpy fin and then sloped away to his tail somewhere under the water.

I took the telescope from my rucksack and trained it on the great grey giant. From nose to tail he was almost as long as our ship. I'd never seen anything so wonderful, and for one fleeting moment his small sad eye seemed to look right at me, making me shiver with excitement. Then, dipping his head below the surface the whale dived again, a tail as wide as a ship's sail lifting high into the air and sliding beneath the waves with a thunderous splash.

'Sharpen your knives, cook,' roared the captain. 'Grub's up! Hoist every sail we've got, you lubbers.' The crew ran to their stations, hoisting extra sails for the chase.

Wow, it's a monster!

Chasing The Whale

A few minutes later the whale surfaced again, further off and heading away from us at top speed.

'Get a move on, you calcified cuttlefish, or we'll lose him!' ordered Cut-throat.

Lizzie Hall took the wheel and turned it towards the whale; the harpooners cranked up their guns, removing the big protective corks from the spears at the same time; Mildew stood grinning over a grinding wheel, sharpening a large machete that sent showers of sparks flying across the deck. The sails filled with a sudden gust of wind and we raced after the monstrous, beautiful whale.

'You can't destroy such a magnificent creature!' I cried to Cut-throat.

'Are you tryin' to tell me what to do, boy?' she exploded, grabbing me by the collar. 'Now, listen up, you worm. *I* am the captain of the *Judgement Day*, not you. I give the orders and everyone else obeys. That's how it works.' And as if I were no heavier than a feather, she lifted me from the deck and held me over the side of the ship, high above the pounding waves. 'Do I make myself clear, you empty-headed anemone?'

'Yeah, I understand,' I squeaked, nodding nineteen-to-the-dozen, and the captain replaced me on the deck.

'Good,' she growled. 'I've no time for your namby-pamby worries. We're going to disembowel and devour that whale, do you hear? His ambergris alone will fill our coffers with gold. The price of his oil will keep us in rum for a year and the steaks will fill our bellies. Now out of my way, sissy, or you'll end up as a garnish on our whale supper.'

The creature sent up another jet of water. We were gaining on it slowly but surely. Despite Cut-throat's threats, I had made up my mind. I wasn't going to stand by and see such a wonderful animal get chopped up for our chow.

But how on earth was I going to save a ten-ton whale?

A Terrible Tale

As I racked my brain for inspiration, Captain Cut-throat paced the deck in a state of uncontained excitement. Then, before I could come up with a single plan to save the whale, she swung up into the rigging and bellowed, 'FIRE!'

With a terrible whistling noise, the pirates shot the harpoons from the guns, *Shoom! Shoom! Shoom!* Trailing long ropes behind them, the harpoons arced through the air towards their target. Two of the deadly spears missed the whale completely, but one embedded itself in the poor creature's blubbery back. The pirate quickly wound the rope around a large cleat and the whale was anchored to the galleon.

The leviathan raised his head and opened his long jaws, letting out an enormous anguished cry. His mouth was big enough to swallow a bus and was lined with teeth as large as kerbstones.

'Oh lovely, we'll get lots of dosh for those choppers as well,' sniggered Annie and the pirates all roared with laughter.

'You pigs!' I cried. 'Why don't you leave him alone?'

'You think that's bad?' said Cut-throat. 'One harpoon is little more than a pinprick to a monster like that. He'll look like a hedgehog before we've finished.'

Not if I've got anything to do with it he won't, I thought.

All of a sudden the whole galleon was jerked forward, sending us toppling to the deck as the huge bull whale accelerated through the waves in a desperate effort to escape. Our ship was dragged along in his wake on the end of the harpoon's long line.

'Hold fast, we're going on a Nantucket sleigh ride,' hooted Captain Cut-throat in excitement. The whale's strong body pulled the *Judgement Day*'s heavy bulk after it, faster and faster, until we were practically skimming over the surface of the sea.

On the ship went, trailing behind the gargantuan fish far across the glittering ocean until, unable to shake us off, the goliath suddenly dived. Deeper and deeper he swam, pulling our galleon's bow under the water after him!

'Shivering swordfish! Prepare to cut the line or we'll all be doomed,' ordered the captain as water began to pour across the deck. Sabre Sue took out her dagger, but just as she went to cut the rope the big bull surfaced, totally exhausted, and our galleon bobbed up safe and sound. Now the poor whale was moving very slowly and we were almost upon him.

'Load the harpoons again,' came Cut-throat's order.

I've got to stop this now, I said to myself, before the poor whale ends up as a floating pincushion. As we came alongside the tiring giant, I checked my rucksack was secure on my back, and then with only half a plan in my head I ran across the deck. Barging past the captain, I grabbed the handle of her gleaming cutlass and drew it from her belt.

'Hey, give that back, you little blister!' bellowed Cut-throat making a grab for me.

But she was too slow.

'Geronimo!' I yelled and leaped over the side, dropping down onto the back of the leviathan poking just above the water.

'Come 'ere, you fool,' yelled the captain. 'What do you think you're playin' at?'

'Whoa!' I cried, sliding across the whale's oily back, straight towards the boiling sea. Yikes! I thought. I'm done for. But at the last minute I managed to grab the harpoon sticking from the creature's thick layers of blubber.

As the pirates lined the deck in surprise and bewilderment, I leaped to my feet and with one mighty slash of the cutlass, sliced through the thick line that joined the whale to the galleon.

Immediately the big bull turned away from the boat, and with renewed energy raced away, with me still clinging to the harpoon. Suddenly he dived, and I was taken down into the seawater with him. We descended towards the ocean's depths until my chest was burning with the need to take a breath, and my ears ached with the pressure.

As we powered still deeper and deeper, the bull whale let out a long, pitiful call that seemed to fill the ocean around us. Then he did a U-turn and raced towards the surface again. I hung on for dear life, blood pounding in my ears and water bubbling around me in foaming silver bubbles.

Above us I saw the dark shadow of the *Judgement Day* getting closer and closer. Oh no, I thought, we're going to ... CRASH! The whale hit the galleon from below. The force of the impact juddered right through his massive body into mine, nearly making me lose my grip on the harpoon.

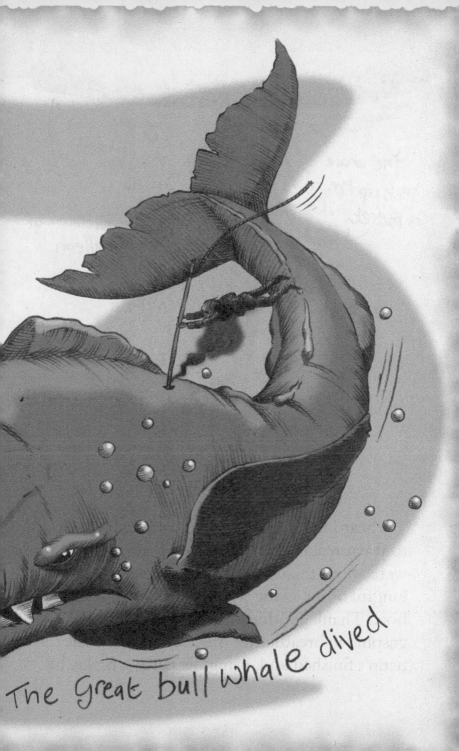

The Great bull whale dived

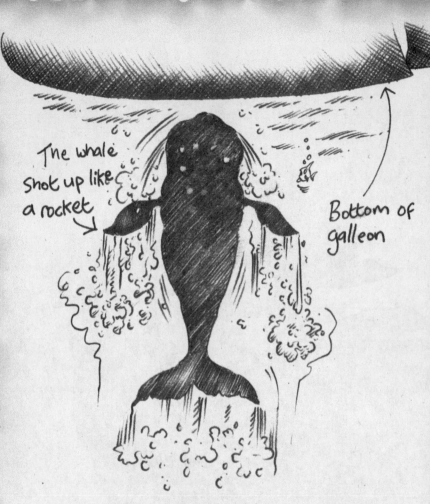

The whale shot up like a rocket

Bottom of galleon

I heard the ripping of metal as the hull started to fracture and then, in a cascade of bubbles, we were above the water again. I gulped in a huge lungful of air as the whale raced away from the boat. Thank goodness that's over, I thought gasping in breath after breath. But the whale hadn't finished and, using his tail as a brake, he turned on a sixpence and went rushing back for another strike.

'Help!' I yelled as we rushed towards the ship like a giant bowling ball hurtling towards a pile of skittles. Suddenly, scores of other whales started popping up from the murky depths and raced alongside us. Were they answering the bull's call? I was now in the middle of a massive marine mammal attack! Harpoons started to rain down at us, fired from guns and thrown by terrified pirates. In their panic though, the sailors lost their aim and the spears fell harmlessly into the sea.

'Stop that thing, Charlie!' yelled the captain, standing on deck amid the shocked faces of her crew, watching as scores of whales raced towards the galleon.

'I don't know where the brakes are!' I shouted back.

BOOM! We hit the galleon again.

BOOM! BOOM! BOOM! Whales attacked from all directions and then *Ping! Ping! Ping!* The rivets holding the *Judgement Day* together started to pop out. Great sheets of metal broke away from the hull.

'Jumping Jellyfish, we're done for! Take to

the lifeboats,' yelled Captain Cut-throat as the sea started to pour in through the gaping holes. Glaring over the side at me, she cried, 'I won't forget this, Charlie Small! You've sunk my unsinkable ship. If we ever meet again I'll open you up like a can of sardines!'

I won't forget this, Charlie Small

'But it's not my fault,' I shouted. 'I'm not steering this thing!'

Before Cut-throat could reply, my bull whale turned away and the *Judgement Day* listed badly in the water. I heard Rawcliffe Annie cry above the sound of ripping metal, 'Hurry up, Cap'n. We've got to go now!'

As the bulky whale turned away with me clutching on to his back, the rusty galleon sank below the waves with a loud gurgle. Oh yikes! I wasn't the biggest fan of the Perfumed Pirates, but I wouldn't wish anyone such a terrible fate. When I looked over my shoulder though, I could see the pirates hauling themselves out of the drink and into long rowing boats. I could faintly hear them arguing, bickering and cursing as they waved their cutlasses in my direction.

Soon they were lost from view, and now, some hours later, I am alone on the ocean on a ginormous bull whale! How the heck am I going to get off here?

A Whale Of A Ride!

I've been sailing across the sea on the monster's back for ages now. It is the strangest means of transport I've been on since starting out on my adventures! The pod of other whales escorted us on our journey for a while; some were great moving mountains of blubber, others quite small, but none were as big as the monster I am on. The whale school swam silently through the waves, the only noise being the splash of fins on water, and the occasional squawk of a seagull.

At first, I didn't know what to think. Was I being taken somewhere? Was the whale even aware that I was sitting on his back, or might he dive down to the bottom of the ocean and leave me floundering in the water?

Although it didn't seem to bother him, I decided I must do something about the dreadful spear sticking out of his back. I got unsteadily to my feet and grabbed hold of the harpoon. Very gently I started to apply pressure and the harpoon moved with a horrible sticky sound. I pulled a bit more and, hey presto, the weapon slid cleanly out of the wound. The whale's back twitched and he smacked his tail onto the surface of the water, but other than that he showed no sign of discomfort.

I threw the harpoon into the sea and have just scooped up some handfuls of seawater to rinse the cut. There is no bleeding, and I know that salt water is a very good cleanser. I'm sure the injury will quickly heal.

My big friendly whale let out a booming cry, and with answering calls all the other whales have disappeared below the surface, leaving just the old bull and me alone on the water. Now the sun has set and the moon has risen in the night sky. I'm sitting quite comfortably at the front of the whale's head, but daren't go to sleep in case I fall into the sea! So, instead I'm keeping myself awake by writing up these notes, while the whale sings a strange and wonderful song of the deep.

The Next Day

The sun has just risen again, warming my aching bones after the chilly night. There is still nothing in sight on the ocean, but I'm keeping my eyes peeled for a passing steamer.

I'm starting to get very hungry. I didn't have time for breakfast on the *Judgement Day* and the last thing I ate was at Jakeman's factory ages ago!

Where on earth are we going?

And The Day After That!

Last night I was so tired that I *did* fall asleep.
The whale must have scooped me out of the
sea when I slid sleepily from his back, because
when I woke up I nearly had a heart attack – I
was lying down on the whale's enormous tongue
inside his cavernous mouth. I thought I was
being eaten alive! But when I let out a cry of
alarm, the gentle giant opened his jaws with a
creak, and I climbed out onto his bottom lip
(thank goodness, because it stank of rotting fish
in there!) The whale then ducked his head below
the water, leaving me doggy paddling on the
surface for a moment, before lifting me out so I
was back on top of his huge, scarred skull again,
where I could dry out in the early morning sun.

'Thanks Whale, I think you might have saved
my life,' I said, patting his wide, oily back, and
he smacked his enormous tail and honked in
response.

As I checked and cleaned the whale's wound
again, I began to think. Eventually my whale
was going to have to dive for food. He would
want to go back to his family. What if we hadn't

Yikes, I'm being eaten by a whale!

found dry land by then? I would be left on my own and might have to swim to safety – and who knows how far that might be! I needed an alternative means of transport. If only I had the right parts I could make myself a raft. I was becoming an expert at raft building!

I decided to keep an eye-out for any bits of flotsam or jetsam floating along in the ocean currents. Hour after hour passed but there was no sign of any useful junk. I began to panic, expecting the whale to dive at any minute, but the faithful old thing kept chugging along! Then, at last, as we passed through a strong current I saw a small collection of rubbish floating towards us. I reached down and made a grab for it.

Brilliant! There was the decapitated head from an ancient teddy bear; a tangle of orange nylon rope; two large plastic containers – and a discarded timber pallet that had probably fallen from a container ship. It was just what I needed. (There was also a handful of fat, bubbly seaweed that I wolfed down. It was delicious!) I got to work on my raft straight away. I put the teddy's head into my rucksack as proof of this incredible journey. Then, using the length of nylon string, I tied the plastic containers to the pallet to give it extra buoyancy. Using the rest of the orange string, I tied one end to the raft and the other around my wrist – now, if the whale dived and left me floundering in the water, I wouldn't lose my makeshift boat. I felt much better and decided to have a little catnap . . .

I've just been woken by a deep, resonant honking call that has set my heart racing. What made the old bull cry out, I wonder; is there a ship coming – and if so, is it friend or foe? I have forced open my bleary eyes, and my heart is now leaping with joy! I can see a faint smudge of land on the horizon! Yippee! I was beginning to think I'd be sailing the seven seas on this whale forever – at last I will be able to stand on solid ground.

I'm just finishing these notes, then I'll get ready to sail to the island. I hope my blubbery friend takes me a bit closer — it's still a long way off. Never mind, things are definitely looking up!

A Fearsome Forest! (Oo-er!)

As the whale swam nearer to the landmass, I could see it was a long peninsula of low-lying land, completely covered in dense forest. It stretched away as far as I could see, disappearing into the misty distance. The foliage was so dark a green as to appear almost black. It looked gloomy and threatening, and I started to feel more than a little scared.

It was the most inhospitable-looking place I've ever seen and a shiver snaked down my backbone. The black forest canopy grew thick and unbroken, climbing in great leafy domes, high above the ground. I'll be better off staying on the whale, I thought to myself, until we discover a friendlier-looking place.

At that very moment, though, the whale trumpeted one last call and slipped below the water. Yikes!

'Hold on, chum,' I cried. I made a grab for the raft and as I clambered onto it the whale's gigantic tail rose out of the sea, waved once in farewell and then slid below the surface.

'Come back, whale,' I cried. 'I don't like the look of this place.' But the whale did not return. I was on my own in the wide, wild sea and the sooner I got ashore the better – my rickety raft was very unstable. I had no choice but to head for the coast!

I started towards land using Captain Cutthroat's cutlass as an oar, but there were strong currents and a heavy swell that made paddling very hard. I was soon puffing and panting as the raft spun in circles and was carried away on tides that took me in completely the wrong direction.

Waves washed over my rickety craft and it started sinking at one corner. As I dug the

cutlass into the sea, paddling furiously, I began
to worry that I wouldn't be able to make it. I
was going backwards! But then a large wave
took hold of my raft and washed me towards
the land. I rode the surf all the way in, right on
to a soft white sandy beach. I'd made it – I was
on solid ground once more!

A Scare On The Beach

I stepped quietly onto the beach, sinking up to
my ankles in fine, silver sand. Pulling the raft
behind me, I left it high up on the beach in case
I needed it for a speedy getaway.

The sun shone down and the deserted sands
were warm under my feet. Little crabs scurried
across the seashore towards the sea, and on a
rock further down the beach stood a puffin, its
beak holding a row of freshly-caught sardines.
But these were the only signs of life, and the air
was ominously quiet.

No sound of birdsong and no animal
cries came from the wall of vegetation that
marked the start of the immense black forest.
Here, thick shrubs and feathery ferns grew

in impenetrable clumps between tall, rough-barked trees whose trunks twisted and coiled grotesquely. The surf sucked at the shore behind me, sounding loud in the silence and I felt very, very alone.

Then I heard the crack of a twig and my heart nearly leaped from my mouth.

'Who's there?' I cried, but there was no response. 'I said, who's there?' I repeated, gripping Cut-throat's cutlass in case an unknown enemy burst from the forest fringe.

Again nobody responded, but then the ferns in front of me started to move and sway violently. I gasped, taking a step back and raising my sword. 'OK. Stop mucking about,' I called in a shaky voice. 'Come out and show yourself.' The ferns shook and shivered and I was just about to fly into an attack, when a wrinkly old turtle pulled itself out of the undergrowth.

'Phew!' I cried, plonking myself down. 'You gave me the fright of my life!' But the turtle just stared at me blankly as it wriggled across the beach, heading for its ocean home.

'Right,' I said out loud to myself. 'What now, Charlie Small?'

Decisions, Decisions!

I'm sitting on the warm sand, writing up my journal and trying to make some plans. It seems to me that I've got two choices: I can either push on into the dark forest and see where it leads, or stay where I am and hope a ship will pass by and pick me up.

I could be waiting for ages for a ship to appear; but if I try and find my way through the forest, it might not lead anywhere at all. I could just end up on another beach, miles further along the wooded peninsula. I can see the forest stretch right down the coast to where it disappears into the mists of the horizon. It seems to go on forever and ever . . . OK, that's decided me! I'll stay close to the beach and build a great big bonfire. If I see a ship out on the ocean, I can light the fire as a distress signal.

Now all I need is something to eat and a safe place to sleep. The sun is already sinking towards the sea and soon it will be dark. In the morning I will explore my new home and build some sort of shelter – I could be living here for some time!

My First Morning

I dined on boiled periwinkles last night. They are a small sea snail and, despite being very chewy, were mighty delicious! Paddling in the shallows of the sea, I found loads of the slithering snails stuck to an outcrop of rock just below the waterline. I pulled a couple of handfuls away and took them back to the beach.

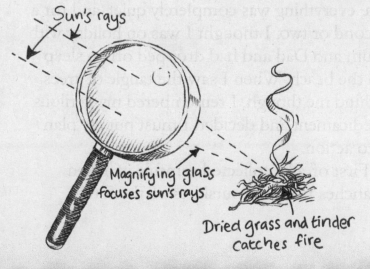

A Periwinkle Yum!

Collecting some dry and dusty tinder wood from the edge of the forest, I built a little mound of brushwood; then, using the magnifying glass from my explorer's kit, I focused the last rays of the sun onto the twigs

Sun's rays

Magnifying glass focuses sun's rays

Dried grass and tinder catches fire

until a little plume of smoke started to rise. Blowing gently, the twigs began to glow until, hooray! tiny flames licked the air.

Down by the ocean's edge I scavenged a large empty conch shell, which I filled with seawater and took back to my fire. Then, resting the shell over the flames, I popped the periwinkles into the water. Before long I was enjoying slimy and salty sea snails for tea! It's amazing what you will eat when you're hungry enough!

Feeling full, I scraped a long depression in the sand, lay down in it, and scooped the sand back down on top of me for a blanket. Nice and warm and with my rucksack for a pillow, I instantly fell into a dreamless sleep.

It took me a while to remember where I was when I awoke. Apart from the sound of the sea, everything was completely quiet, and for a second or two, I thought I was on holiday with Mum and Dad and had dropped off to sleep on the beach. When I saw the tangle of trees behind me though, I remembered my perilous predicament and decided I must put my plan into action.

First of all I collected armfuls of fallen branches from the outskirts of the forest, dumping them into a big pile in the middle of the beach. Then I added a covering of green leaves, which I knew would

The beacon!

create lots of dense smoke. Now, if a ship passes by I can fire up the beacon with my magnifying glass. There's no way anyone would miss it. I need to take care of my magnifying glass. If I lose it I'll have to resort to rubbing two sticks together to produce a flame. That can take ages and by the time a decent blaze got going, any rescue ship might have disappeared over the horizon!

Next I built a shelter. The best place, I decided, would be up in the trees near the edge of the forest. From there I could look out over the ocean and also be safe from any prowling predators. I still don't know if there are any prowling predators around. It certainly

doesn't seem
like it – the
woods are
still as silent
as a cathedral –
but it's better to
be safe than wake up with
your leg in the mouth of a
big, bad wolf!

Good
morning!

House Hunting

Putting on my rucksack, I took a deep breath
and pushed my way into the thick undergrowth
at the edge of the forest. I struggled and barged
as thorns and branches snagged my clothes and
scratched my hands. Jeepers, it was tough work
– like trying to crawl through a coil of barbed
wire. Eventually though, with one big heave, I
broke through the wall of bushes.

If the forest looked scary from the outside, it
looked a hundred times scarier now! It was very,
very gloomy, with only a weak light filtering
down from above. The ground was covered
with a patchwork of moss and grass, clumps of

silver-leafed ferns and thick, gnarly tree roots that snaked and branched every which way across the forest floor.

The trunks of the trees rose thick and black in every direction, some growing straight up like pillars in a church, others contorted into the most fantastic shapes. All around me, the forest disappeared into a murky distance. It was the sort of place where you expected a witch to pop out at any minute, and although I don't believe in witches or ghouls, my heart started to beat faster and my mouth went dry.

Are there witches in the forest?

'Don't be such a wimp,' I said to myself, and my voice sounded muffled and lost amongst the trees. 'There's nothing here to harm you, not even a tiny woodlouse! Now get on with what you came to do.'

I wandered through the trees, when all of a sudden I realized that if I wasn't careful I wouldn't be able to find my way back to the beach and my beacon. Somehow, I needed to mark my route. I kicked away a covering of decomposing leaves on the ground and turned over a few rocks with the toe of my trainer. Aha! That would do. I picked up a large pebble of white, chalky stone and drew a big X on the trunk of the nearest tree. Feeling happier, I carried on, marking my way every few metres with a new X.

The trees grew so close together that sometimes it was a tight fit to squeeze in between their mossy trunks, but I soon came to a place that was more open; where the sun pushed through the leaves overhead in soft shafts of pale light. In the middle of the clearing was the perfect tree for my shelter.

It was tall – very tall, and thrust its way through the branches of the surrounding trees and out above their canopies. There weren't any side branches that I could climb on to for about eight or ten metres, but, taking the lasso from my rucksack, I span it around my head and let it go. It caught a branch and I pulled the rope to tighten the noose, and then shinned up until I could grab a bough and haul myself into the tree.

For a boy who's spent years amongst a pack

of wild gorillas, it was an easy task to climb the rest, and soon I was in the swaying topmost branches, looking out over the wide, wild ocean in one direction and the endless, wild forest in the other. The perfect location!

Home, Sweet Home!

I started to build a shelter by sawing off long, straight branches with the megashark's tooth from my explorer's kit. I bound the branches together with strips of tough fern stems that I carried up in a bundle from the ground, and soon I had built a platform resting in a wide, forked limb in the tree. Next, I forced sticks into the tight gaps between the branches of the platform.

Between these I wove thin, whippy shoots to create the walls and topped the whole thing off with layers of wide leaves for a roof. Lastly, I fixed my telescope to a branch, facing out to sea to keep a lookout for boats and, even if I say so myself, the whole thing looked pretty fantastic! By the time I'd put down a pile of dry, crackly leaves for a bed, it was a real home from home.

My brilliant treehouse

With my shelter built, I climbed down to the ground and went in search of some grub! After all my hard work I was feeling really hungry, but didn't fancy eating winkles again unless I had to. My tummy has been bubbling ominously all day!

Drawing Xs en route, I went in search of berries or mushrooms or anything that looked remotely edible. I was still very wary and carried my cutlass at the ready. But the forest just went on and on, silent as the grave, with no birds clattering and chattering overhead; no squirrels or foxes creeping through the undergrowth and no rabbits running for cover as twigs snapped under my feet. It was mighty weird. Why was the forest so empty?

At last I found a large bank of bramble bushes hanging with blackberries, and I stuffed my mouth with the sharp fruit until the juice ran down my chin. It helped, but it wasn't enough and I returned to my treehouse still feeling hungry.

I'm completely exhausted now, but feel very safe in my little house in the roof of the forest. I'm sprawled out on the comfy bed of leaves, drinking from my water bottle that I filled from a shallow rain puddle. My journal's up to date and now I *must* get some sleep – I hope I don't fall out of this tree in the middle of the night!

Good riddance to Captain Cut-throat
P _ R _ T E
B C
F H G
O S K N
Z
Is anybody there?

The Judgement Day goes to a watery grave!
Will I ever see Jakeman again?
Pirates, grrr!
Will I ever get out of this silent forest?
A Leaf from my tree
wonder what all my
hool friends are doing?
Double maths, I hope!)

Things Start To Happen!

Over the following days I did more work to my shelter, adding a small balcony and building a little wooden chair to sit on. I made plates out of wood and a fork from a sturdy, pronged twig; I kept a sharp lookout for ships, and made further sorties into the deep, dark forest, but I didn't find any signs of life.

My plate and fork

At night I would sometimes take out the little wooden box Philly had given me and wonder what she and Jakeman were up to. Had they managed to free themselves from their ropes; were they scouring the ocean for me in their hover-sub at that very moment? If they were, I never caught sight of them. The sea remained empty and the forest spookily quiet and I knew that if a ship didn't pass by soon, I would have to pack up my rucksack and try and navigate my way through the vast forest of towering trees.

I'm starting to feel like Robinson Crusoe, one of my favourite adventure heroes. I've made a thick jacket of moss for the chilly evenings and my hair has grown halfway down to my shoulders! If I could grow a beard like Robinson, it would be about three metres long by now!

My meals are a bit boring. I have stinky boiled cabbage for breakfast, dinner and tea! It grows on the edge of the forest and, when cooked in salty seawater, doesn't taste too bad. The worst thing is that it gives you chronic wind. Phwoar! I could have steamed crab, a delicacy I'd learned to cook when I was with the Perfumed Pirates the first time around. There are plenty of the nippy little things crawling about the beach, but I don't have the heart to drop them in the pot!

Then, just this morning, something happened that changed everything. I was out exploring when a heart-stopping, ear-piercing scream came from the depths of the black forest!

It echoed in the still air and the blood ran cold in my veins, making me shudder and my knees wobble. What the heck was that? I obviously wasn't alone after all! My first instinct was to run to the safety of my treehouse, but as an intrepid explorer I knew it was my duty to find out what had made such an unearthly sound.

A Wall Of Skulls!

Twigs cracked under my feet as I went deeper into the forest than I'd ever been before. I crept through the wild wood with Cut-throat's cutlass in my hand. Everything had gone quiet again as I trudged in the direction of the scream. Then I caught a faint whiff in the air. As I carried on, the smell got stronger. It was like the horrible sour pong of rotting manure, and my eyes began to smart. What was it? I wondered. I was sure I'd smelled it before. But where?

Turning a corner I suddenly found myself in a sort of amphitheatre. Great granite pillars covered in intricate and ancient carvings were arranged in a large semi-circle. In the centre of the enclosure stood a raised stone dais covered in bloodstains. Beyond that was a wall, five metres high, made of thousands upon thousands of *bleached white skulls*!

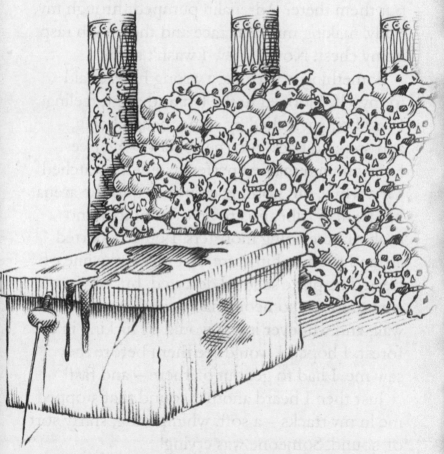

'Oh, cripes!' I whispered. It was horrific. Empty eyes stared silently back at me from countless skulls, both animal and human, which seemed to mock me with their ghastly toothy grins. What were they doing here, piled up so neatly? And what was more worrying – who had put them there? Adrenalin pumped through my body, making my heart race and the breath rasp in my chest. Now I knew I wasn't alone!

Something is very, very wrong here, I said to myself. I looked to the left and right, feeling I was being watched by some malign being, and stepped back into the cover of the trees. Everything remained perfectly quiet. I watched for a while, but nothing crept out into the arena. No terrible tribe, no crowd of cannibals, no mob of screaming monsters. I quietly skirted around the amphitheatre, just inside the line of trees. The place seemed deserted, but obviously something or someone had built that grisly wall, and whoever it was would be lurking in the forest. I hoped I would see them before they saw me. I had to get out of there – and fast!

Just then I heard another sound that stopped me in my tracks – a soft, whimpering, sniffy sort of sound. Someone was crying!

Knee-high

I noiselessly tiptoed over to some scrubby undergrowth and peered over the top.

At first I didn't see anything. Then, as the creature sniffed again, I saw it. Half-covered by a large fern leaf and stretched out in a small hollow in the rich, dark soil, was a little mole. He was gently sobbing into his front paws, looking lost and all alone.

I didn't want to startle the animal, but a twig snapped beneath my feet and the animal gasped and looked up. Seeing me peering over the bush, he squeaked and held up his large paws as if to ward off a blow.

'Don't worry little chap,' I said quietly. 'I'm not going to harm you. What are you crying for, anyway? Has somebody hurt you?'

The mole tried to scurry away, but I managed to catch him by his thick, black velvet fur and lifted him from the ground. His stubby little legs continued running in mid air like a clockwork toy!

'Sshhh,' I said and cradled the animal in my arms. I stroked the top of his head, and immediately the mole calmed down, a look of sleepy pleasure filling his tiny black eyes.

I popped him back on the ground. 'I won't hurt you,' I said again. 'What's your name?' He peeped forlornly, and I felt stupid. Just because I could speak gorilla and had met talking trees and owls, I expected every animal to be able to talk to me. This little chap obviously couldn't. Never mind. Perhaps I could learn to talk mole as well!

He peeped again, pointing over towards the clearing where the wall of skulls stood. 'Peep, peep, peep,' he said excitedly.

'What are you trying to warn me about?' I asked. 'What are you so scared of?'

'Peep, peep,' he said again. Then, picking up a twig from the ground, the mole scratched something in the soft soil. This is what he drew:

'That's a rat!' I cried. 'Rats built that horrific wall?'

'Peep!' he replied.

Then I remembered where I'd smelled that horrible odour before. It was in the Underworld, where I had been knocked down by a stampede of subterranean rats! Were these the same species? And if so, what were they doing here?

'You'd better come home with me,' I said to the mole. 'You look lost, and it's too dangerous around here.' I put out my hand, and the trusting animal went to take it. Then he remembered something, and toddling back to the bush where I found him, he reached in and pulled out what looked like a gruesome headless body!

'Peep,' he piped, holding the limp torso up to me.

'Ugh!' I gasped. 'That's horrible.' But then I saw what it was – the mole was holding up the headless body of a worn and threadbare teddy. He held it up to his cheek and cuddled it with a look of bliss. Then he started peeping angrily, and pointed in the direction of the skull wall.

'What, the rats did that to your toy?' I asked.

'Peep,' said the mole mournfully. I don't think he knew what I was saying, but we seemed to understand each other well enough. All of a sudden I remembered what I had in my rucksack! I pulled out the teddy's head I'd fished from the ocean and handed it to the mole. He peeped in excitement, jumping up and down, kissing the decapitated head and talking to it in little clicks and grunts.

Then he happily took hold of my hand with his large, spade-shaped paw and we wandered off through the trees, following the X marks I had made. The little mole only came up to my knee, and as I couldn't ask his name, I decided to call him Knee-high. 'Come on, Knee-high,' I said. 'Let's go home and get some grub.'

Even though I couldn't understand a word, Knee-high peeped and squeaked all the way back to the treehouse. He seemed so happy to have found his teddy and made a new friend. I was really pleased to have some company as well; I'd been on my own in the forest for weeks, and was starting to go a bit doolally!

Peep!

All the way home, though, I had the uncomfortable feeling we were being watched. Had the smelly rats heard us? Were they stealthily stalking us through the forest? There was no rustling in the undergrowth and I didn't see any beady eyes peering from behind the trees; I just had a horrible sensation that we weren't alone. I gripped the cutlass in my belt. If they tried anything I was ready for them!

I felt safer when I'd carried Knee-high up to

the treehouse, hoping that if the rats really had followed us they wouldn't be able to climb to the top of our tree. I decided to put off trying to find an escape route through the forest until I was sure they weren't still hanging around. I didn't want to run into them and have *my* bonce added to their gruesome wall!

My Little Helper

Now we've been home for a few days, and Knee-high has proved to be a very useful companion. I roughly sewed the raggedy head back onto the teddy's body with a bit of string from my explorer's kit. The mole was delighted, and is so grateful to me for taking him in that he has insisted on doing most of the housework. I don't want him to, of course – seeing him scurrying around and tidying up after me, has made me feel just a little bit mean. But the tiny chap will not stop!

In the mornings, as I keep a watch on the ocean for ships and the forest for rats, Knee-high shakes up the leaves of my bed and then, using the seed head of a huge dandelion-like plant, he dusts around my small shack. After that he digs a new latrine in the woods and covers up the old one with soil. (I'm secretly glad he takes on *this* task, as it's a really smelly job!) With those duties done, we go down to the beach and Knee-high cooks me breakfast.

He's shown me where I can pick blackberries, which mushrooms are safe to eat, and even how I can grind up certain seeds to make a stodgy sort of boiled bread. This morning, when he produced a crusty covered pie of chopped worms though, I drew the line. No matter how hungry I get, I will never ever ever eat worms!

Two Days Later

I tried worm pie for the first time! (The blackberries and mushrooms have run out.) It was delicious, a bit like chicken, but I don't advise anyone else trying it unless an expert mole cooks it!

Worm pie

yum, yum!

A Ship! A Ship!

I was up and about very early this morning, and as Knee-high busied himself around our home I took a cup of herb tea out onto the balcony. The canopy of trees rolled out below me like great billowing dark clouds, all the way to the narrow beach. Beyond, the ocean stretched from horizon to horizon, gleaming like silver in the weak morning light – and slap bang in the middle was a big steam ship!

'At last!' I yelled, and my voice echoed over the treetops.

'Peep?' enquired the mole, coming out to see what all the fuss was about.

'A ship, Knee-high, a ship!' I cried. 'At last I'm going to be rescued. Look!'

I lifted the little animal up so he could see the liner. It was bright blue against the shimmering water, with one big funnel pumping out plumes of white smoke that sat motionless in the

still air. What a beautiful sight, I thought.

'Come on, Knee-high. We're wasting time!' I
said and, grabbing my rucksack, and lifting my
little friend onto my shoulders, began to climb
down through the spreading branches of our
tree. I kept the lasso coiled up on a bough to
stop anything climbing up to our treehouse. I
pushed it off its branch so it snaked away to the
ground, wrapped my legs around it and slid all
the way down.

I ran through the forest and barged through
the curtain of bramble onto the beach.
Dropping onto my knees in front of the big
bonfire, I took out my magnifying glass and
trained it onto the dry twigs at the bottom.

'Come on, hurry up!' I said but nothing
happened. The ship was already chugging past
us, turning away from the forest headland.
Looking back at the magnifying glass, I willed
the twigs to start smoking. 'Come on you useless
thing, why aren't you working!' I glared up at the
sky, and realized why I wasn't getting a flame.
The sun was hidden behind a long wispy cloud.
The beams weren't strong enough to start a fire!

'Dash, drat and double darn it!' I yelled, and
Knee-high scampered behind the bonfire to

hide. 'Sorry, Knee-high,' I sighed. 'I didn't mean to scare you.'

I checked the cloud and the position of the ship again. It was no good – the cloud was too big and the ship would be gone before the sun came out. Unbelievable – it was the first bloomin' cloud I'd seen since I got here!

There was nothing for it; I would have to try rubbing two sticks together. I grabbed some twigs from the edge of the forest, but when I returned to the beach I knew it was hopeless. The ship was already sailing from view.

'Come back,' I yelled, jumping up and down and waving my arms in the air. 'Hey, come back, *please*!' But the ship carried on. Soon it was just a speck on the horizon and I knew I'd missed my chance. I threw the sticks on the ground in disgust and returned to the treehouse, feeling totally deflated.

I've been in a bad mood all day and Knee-high has been keeping out of my way! I'm FED UP, and am not going to write anything else in this journal until something good happens!

An Amazing Find!

Something good *has* happened!

I hadn't smelled any rats since discovering the skull wall, so I decided to venture a bit further into the forest to look for fresh food supplies. I was walking along a wide, leafy track with my mole chum, when I spotted something glinting amongst the undergrowth.

'Down!' I cried, dropping to my knees behind the buttressed trunk of a massive tree. 'I think I saw a rat's eye!' Knee-high peeped and hid behind me.

Very quietly, I peered around the tree. Yes, there was definitely something hiding in the brush. I'd brought my telescope with me and, taking it from my rucksack, trained it on the bushes. I could make out an eye; part of a huge domed back and . . . a finned exhaust pipe?

'I don't believe it!' I cried, getting to my feet and rushing over to the gorse.

'Peep!' cried Knee-high in warning. 'Peep, peep!'

'Don't worry,' I said, tearing back the branches. 'I think I know what this is!'

I cleared the brambles out of the way, and there in the middle of the bush was a massive metal beast.

'I thought so,' I cried. 'It's one of Jakeman's inventions – some sort of armoured animal. It looks as powerful as a tank. Oh, brilliant! I might be able to drive it straight through the forest and out the other side! Good old Jakeman and his marvellous mechanimals! Come on, Knee-high, let's have a proper look.'

We cleared away as many branches as we could, but the more of the machine we uncovered the scruffier it looked. Knee-high stared at it, looking confused. He didn't seem very impressed with my find!

'It must have been here for ages,' I said, a bit disappointed. There was a lot of rust on the joints and thick bindweed coiled on the creature's metal legs. It was as run-down as an ancient tractor in the forgotten corner of a farmer's barn. 'Never mind, Knee-high. We can do her up. I wonder if there are any instructions anywhere?'

I climbed up onto the big domed back of the machine. In the top was a wide cavity, with a long leather-covered seat for a driver. Two levers stuck up from the floor with brake handles on the end and there was a big, flat accelerator pedal between them. I felt along the shelf under the fascia and almost immediately my hand closed around a sheet of paper.

'Aha!' I cried. 'This is what I need.' It was the mechanimal's specification sheet, and it's amazing: (See the drawing on the next page)

What a fantastic-looking machine, I thought. Surely I'll be able to batter my way through the thickest, prickliest undergrowth in this monster!

APPROVED JAKEMAN MECHANIMAL

Jakeman

IF IT DOESN'T HAVE MY SIGNATURE
IT WASN'T MADE BY ME

ACCEPT NO INFERIOR SUBSTITUTES

Gunge Gun

Steel shell

Flashing
eyes

Armour-
plated
head

Offensive claws

Jakeman's Petrol-driven Armoure

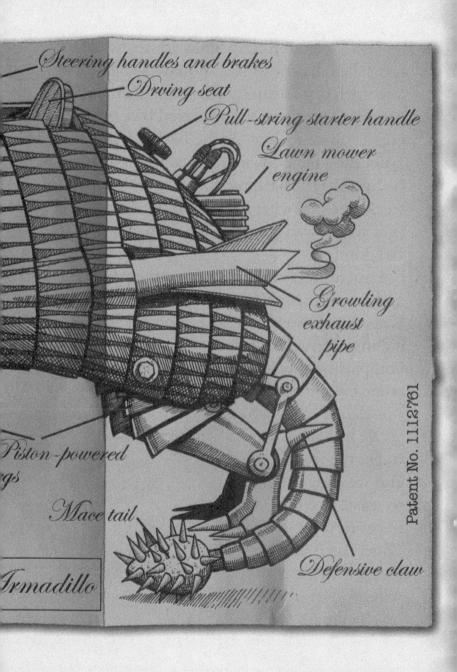

Steering handles and brakes

Drving seat

Pull-string starter handle

Lawn mower engine

Growling exhaust pipe

Piston-powered legs

Mace tail

Defensive claw

Irmadillo

Patent No. 1112761

The Armoured Armadillo, for that's what
it is called, has powerful shoulders encased in
a tempered steel sheet. The head is similarly
protected, and pistons, powered by a petrol
engine, drive its legs. At the back, a long
articulated tail ends in a spiked mace that would
be brilliant for bashing down medium-sized
trees. It is just what I need! Forget being saved
by a ship. I want to drive the Armadillo to
freedom!

I got a shock when I opened the petrol cap
and found the tank was as dry as a bone, but
Knee-high's powerful nose soon smelled out
a dump of fuel cans deeper in the bush. In a
compartment under the dashboard I also found
some oil and spanners and a
booklet of instructions.

We have all we need
to get the thing going
and we aren't going
to waste any time. I
have started rubbing
down the Armadillo's
joints with a ball of
wire wool from the
mechanimal's toolkit.

Knee-high wants to help, though I'm not sure he knows what he is doing, or why!

Yahoo! At last, things are definitely looking up!

Phoning Home!

It's night-time now, and I'm just finishing writing up my journal. I'm sure it won't be long before I escape this forest and that's made me think about home. If I get back to Jakeman's Factory as quickly as possible, and if his Archway to Anywhere works, I could soon be back in my own world. I rang Mum a few minutes ago, to tell her to expect me.

For her it's still the same Sunday I set out on my adventures and she's still expecting me back in time for tea – even though I know I've been gone for four hundred years! How does that work? I must have crossed over into another time zone or something. Anyway, every time I ring her, she always says the same thing.

'Oh, hello darling, is everything all right?' Mum asked when she lifted the receiver.

'Sort of, Mum,' I said. 'I've been stuck in a deep, dark forest for ages. There's a massive wall made of millions of skulls here, and I think I can smell rats!'

'Ooh! That sounds nice, dear,' said Mum. 'Just make sure you don't catch cold.'

'Mum!' I cried. 'Did you hear what I said?'

'Oh, wait a minute, Charlie. Here's your dad just come in. Now remember, don't be late for tea and pick up a carton of milk on the way home.'

'Yes, Mum,' I sighed as the line went dead. These phone calls to Mum are really frustrating, but it's good to hear her voice when I'm so far away from home.

I put the phone on the floor and tipped the rest of the contents of my rucksack out beside it. If I plan on riding the Armadillo to freedom, I'd better check my precious explorer's kit – things that have helped me time after time on my dangerous adventures. I would never go anywhere without it. If you ever want to do some exploring, make sure you take a bag full of useful things as well. My rucksack now contains:

1) My multi-tooled penknife
2) A ball of string
3) A water bottle

4) A telescope (tied to a branch outside)
5) A scarf (complete with bullet holes!)
6) An old railway ticket
7) This journal
8) A pack of wild animal collectors cards (full of fantastic animal facts)
9) A glue pen to stick things in my notebook with
10) A glass eye from the brave steam-powered rhinoceros   See my Journal Gorilla City
11) The compass and torch I found on the sun-bleached skeleton of a lost explorer
12) The tooth of a monstrous megashark

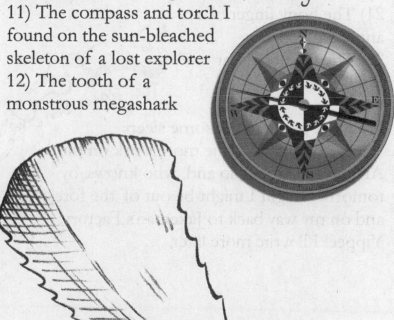

13) A magnifying glass
14) A radio
15) My mobile phone with wind-up charger
16) The skull of a Barbarous Bat
17) A bundle of maps collected during
my travels
18) A bag of marbles
19) A plastic lemon full of lemon juice
20) A lasso (also tied to a branch so I can climb
up into my treehouse)
21) The bony finger of an
animated skeleton
22) The little box that
Philly gave me

The finger bone

Now I'm going to get some sleep.
Tomorrow I'll do some more work on the
Armoured Armadillo and, who knows, by
tomorrow night I might be out of the forest
and on my way back to Jakeman's Factory.
Yippee! I'll write more later.

RAT AMBUSH!

I'm NOT out of the forest. I'm NOT on my way to the factory. I'm in the most perilous position I've been in since starting out on my adventures. I don't believe it! Why do these things always happen to me?

Knee-high and I were up and about early the next morning. I had a quick wash in the sea and combed my hair with a dried-up anemone. Then we tramped through the forest, following the X marks I'd made on the trees. As soon as we reached the Armadillo, we started polishing and oiling, tightening bolts and cleaning connections.

At one point I thought I caught a faint ratty whiff in the air, and noticed Knee-high's snout was nervously twitching and sniffing. Were the mysterious rodents out and about?

I tried to glean more information from my little furry friend – who were these rats? Why was he so scared of them, and why was the forest so strangely empty? But every question I asked, Knee-high would take up a stick and draw the same picture of a rat.

'Yes, you *told* me there are rats here,' I cried, getting frustrated. 'But what about them? What have they done?'

Again the mole drew a rat in the sand, but this time he drew a big X next to it. Then he did another sketch.

'Hello, what's that?' I asked. 'It looks like a badger!' Next to this, Knee-high drew a big tick.

'Rats bad, badgers good?' I asked. 'Is that what you mean?'

'Peep!' said the mole.

'But there aren't any badgers,' I protested. 'I haven't even seen any rats for that matter. For all I really know, you're the only other living thing in this forest apart from me!' But I knew from the terrible wall of skulls and the fetid stench in the air that this couldn't be true. No, I hadn't seen any rats, but they were definitely there . . . as I was just about to find out!

We packed up for the day, and I was confident that I would be able to start up the Armadillo the next morning and give it a test drive. Then, walking back towards our treehouse, the terrible, throat-burning stench filled the air around us, much, much stronger than ever before.

'Peep!' cried Knee-high, running around in a panic. 'Peep, peep, peep!'

'Rats?' I asked.

'Peeeeep!' he whistled, just as a troop of ten greasy brown rats leaped out of the undergrowth in front of us; rats as big as dogs, standing on their hind legs and brandishing evil-looking foils. But not only were there rats – among them were some elongated, writhing weasels with eyes as red as blood and teeth like pins.

'*Neeeep!*' the animals screamed in piercing squeals as they started to form a circle around us, jabbing the air with their foils. 'Neeep, neeeep!' I knew I had to act quickly, before we were completely surrounded and, grabbing Knee-high with my left hand, I swung him onto my shoulders. With my right hand, I drew my cutlass, swishing it before me, stopping the rats and weasels in their tracks.

One of the Wily Weasels

'Get back, you vermin,' I yelled in my best piratey voice. 'Get back or I'll slice you into slivers and serve you up for me tea!'

But either they didn't understand or they weren't in the least bit impressed. They didn't get back at all – instead they came forwards, jabbing at my legs with their needle-sharp swords. I parried and thrust and counter-attacked with my cutlass as the pests surged towards us.

I was sure this ghastly gang of guttersnipes must be a highly-ordered patrol of soldiers and I guessed that the troop's commander was the largest and ugliest ratty specimen standing a little way away. In height he came up to my waist and had a long, crooked snout and protruding, discoloured teeth. His scaly and flaky tail swished in the air behind him and his tiny black eyes glowed with hatred.

Ratso –
Commander
of the smelly
rats

The troops attacked again, diving at me and scratching at my legs with their razor-sharp claws, nipping my flesh with their horrible teeth. It was clear the rats were in charge, for the weasels stayed towards the rear, slinking back and forth, hissing and spitting like mad things.

'Yeow! Get off!' I screamed, shaking the rats away and kicking out at them. It felt like I was being stung by a swarm of killer wasps! Then, remembering the windmill technique taught me by Sabre Sue, I span my cutlass in the air like a propeller and charged them at full speed.

The rats and their weaselly pals squealed in fear, running for cover as I ran around like a demented aeroplane, my cutlass swirling in front of me. But at one point Knee-high clung on to me around the face, blocking my eyes with his big paws!

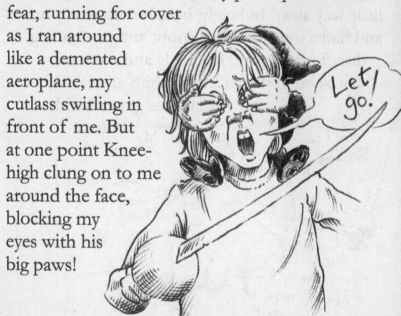

Let go.

'Let go, Knee-high,' I cried blindly, and he adjusted his grip just as I was about to career headlong into a tree. I span around, but luckily our attackers were already in retreat. Shrieking and screeching, the stinking animals disappeared into the undergrowth, following their creepy commander. As the rodents crashed through the bush, the noise got fainter and their smell drifted away. Knee-high and I were left on our own, our hearts drumming loudly.

'Right, that's it. There's no way I'm waiting until tomorrow – let's get out of here now! Do you want to come with me, Knee-high?' I asked the trembling mole, placing him back on the ground.

'Peep!' said the little animal emphatically, though I'm not sure he understood what I meant. But I wasn't leaving him to his fate in the forest.

'To the Armoured Armadillo!' I cried.

Escape Into Danger!

We hurriedly retraced our steps, listening all the time for returning rats. Maybe they had gone to get reinforcements; perhaps they would ambush us again at any minute – but we didn't see, hear or smell anything of them and we were soon back at the Armoured Armadillo.

I hurriedly searched through my rucksack and found my Animal Collectors Cards. Could they tell me anything useful about our attackers?

PREDATOR RATING 8

Giant Rat

If you think ordinary rats are revolting, wait until you meet a giant one! Over a metre in length, they are quick, strong, clever, extremely vicious and very, very smelly.

When they work in packs they can easily overpower creatures much bigger than themselves, biting with germ-infested fangs and ripping with their needle-sharp claws. Don't ever turn your back on a vile Giant Rat!

WILD ANIMAL COLLECTORS CARDS

Well, it didn't tell me anything I hadn't already worked out for myself! I put the cards back in my pack and turned my attention to the Armadillo.

Knee-high helped me pull away the loose branches we'd used to camouflage the machine and then, taking one of the petrol cans, I jumped onto its back, undid the cap and poured the fuel inside. The tank took all six cans and I hoped it would be enough to get us out of the forest.

Grabbing hold of the starter handle, I tugged as hard as I could. The engine coughed and spluttered and stopped. I tried again, and with a bang an oily black cloud plumed from the exhaust. 'Come on, you stupid thing, I'm in a hurry,' I said and gave the engine a kick. Dad used to do that to our lawn mower when it wouldn't start! I gave the string a third pull and, lo and behold, the engine wheezed and glugged and roared into life.

'*Yee-hah!*' I yelled. 'Come on, Knee-high, it's time to go!' I jumped into the driver's seat and the little mole perched beside me. Revving the accelerator, I gripped a lever in each hand and pushed them forward, as the manual had said.

For a second, nothing happened. Then with a terrible grating sound, like a thousand nails being scraped down a blackboard, the Armadillo lumbered forward like an inebriated elephant.

'Result!' I cried and, using first one lever and then the other, steered the machine towards the undergrowth. As the Armadillo ground into action, the oil in its joints started working and the terrible grating noise stopped. With a *CRASH!* we ploughed into the bushes, snapping branches and trampling down plants.

'Hold on tight, Knee-high. It's going to be a bumpy ride!' I shouted above the noise of the engine, and the poor little terrified animal gripped the edge of his seat as he bounced up and down like a furry jack-in-the-box!

I had soon mastered the simple controls of the Armoured Armadillo, but our path was pretty treacherous and sometimes we nearly toppled over as it bumped and shuddered across the rough ground. I needed all my concentration to control it. I drove for miles through the dark, endless forest. I was just about to ask Knee-high whether he wanted to stop and pick a snack when, *WHOOSH!* a heavy net dropped on my head from the trees above.

A net dropped from the tree above!

'Yikes!' I cried, struggling against the mesh, but the more I struggled the more entangled I became. It must be the rats, I thought. They've come back for us! The netting got caught around the levers and I lost control of the Armadillo. With a juddering thump we smashed into a tree and the engine whined in protest, spluttered and died.

I started to clamber out, but when I leaped up from the seat my legs got tangled up and I landed on the ground in a heap, completely covered in the net. Oh flip!

Badgers!

'Let me go, you vermin,' I yelled struggling to free myself. The netting obscured my view, but I caught a glimpse of some heavy bodies thumping to the ground from the trees. They're not the giant rats, I thought. They're much too big and heavy.

'Get 'im boys,' I heard a gruff, fruity voice exclaim.

Immediately, I felt long-clawed paws tugging at the net; then my head popped free and I could see my attackers for the first time. I was surrounded by a gang of enormous thuggish-looking badgers!

'Hang on, what's going on?' I spluttered. 'I thought badgers were meant to be the good guys!'

'Be quiet, you dirty rat!' said the biggest badger. He was almost as tall as me, had a long, powerful muzzle, and wide, sloping muscular shoulders. His gigantic paws ended in terrible-looking claws and he wore a patch over one eye. He menacingly slapped a vicious-looking club into the palm of one paw over and over again.

'*I'm* not a rat,' I cried. 'I'm Charlie Small!'

'Don't try and kid me,' growled the badger. 'Oi can smell a rat a mile away, and ol' Barcus's nose *never* lies.' How come this badger was speaking human? I wondered. And he sounded like an old yokel farmer. It was bizarre!

Barcus came closer, sniffing the air until his muzzle was right in my face. He gave a long sniff. 'Ugh, disgustin'!' he said, wrinkling his nose. 'You're a rat. A bald scrawny-looking rat, but a rat nonetheless.'

'So much for your nose. I am *not* a rat,' I yelled. 'As a matter of fact I've just fought with a load of rats. Perhaps you can smell them on me. Tell him, Knee-high.' I looked around for the mole and it was only then I realized that he was lost. 'Oh no! Where's Knee-high?' I groaned.

'You lookin' for someone?' asked the badger warily.

'A mole! I had a mole with me,' I said. 'He could verify my story.'

'Oh yes? A mole that seems to 'ave mysteriously vanished? A likely story!' said Barcus, with a hollow laugh. 'Oi've heard enough. Men, take this bald rat back to the sett. We'll deal with him there!'

'You're making a mistake,' I protested as two of the badgers slipped a long branch through

the net. They lifted me from the ground and carried me between them down a narrow track that led into the thickest part of the forest.

'Let me go!' I demanded, but my struggles were in vain. I was trapped like a rat in a sack!

At The Badger's Sett

The big beasts carried me along overgrown paths that wound through the forest like a maze. We turned left and right, double-backing and ducking into tracks hidden by hanging branches. Eventually, we came to a wide area of soft, dry soil surrounded by some of the biggest trees I've ever seen. Their branches spread widely overhead, thick with foliage, casting the place into a quiet gloom.

A series of large mounds, like miniature hills, stretched across the whole of the far side of the clearing, and in every mound was a wide hole that led into the ground. The badgers marched across to the mini hills, ducked into one of the holes and, still carrying me, took me down a long passage until we emerged into a high, circular room.

The den was as large as a school hall, quite
bare, with a big domed ceiling and openings
leading off every wall. Sitting on stools in
groups all around the chamber were many more
badgers. Mums and dads were quietly chatting;
some were whittling sticks and others fashioning
clubs out of heavy branches. On the floor, their
cubs argued and laughed and rolled about, play-
fighting. When they saw us, everyone became
quiet and stopped what they were doing. As
Barcus made his way to a tall chair on the other
side of the room, I was dumped on the ground
and the net was pulled off me. I got to my feet
and looked nervously around.

'Rat, rat, rat,' hissed the badger clan. 'Rat, rat,
rat, rat!'

'I am not a rat, I am a *boy*,'
I bellowed. I'd had enough
of this. I mean, really! Fancy
mistaking me for a putrid,
smelly rodent!

I don't look anything like a rat-do I?

'QUIET!' roared Barcus
from his carved wooden throne,
and the room became silent. Then, looking at
me he said, 'We know you're a rat! We can smell
you're a rat, so stop this silly game.'

'But–' I began.

'Oi! I said SILENCE!' the badger roared
again. 'You're on trial for your life. And don't
expect any leniency 'ere, after what you've done.'

'What am I supposed to have done?' I asked.

'With no warning, you and your smelly pack
attacked us in our 'omes and drove us out of
our ancient setts. You killed countless of our
brothers and used their skulls to build your
ghastly wall o' death. You broke the natural
order of the forest,' growled the badger, fixing
me with his one good eye. 'Now all our forest
friends, the birds and rabbits, the foxes and
moles, have gone, driven to the edge of the
wood,' he continued. 'Only the wicked weasels
surrendered and joined your cause. But that's no

surprise – those traitorous vermin will change sides at the drop of a hat. What do you have to say in your defence?'

'I am not a bloomin' rat!' I pleaded.

'Ain't that just typical of a sneaking, two-faced rodent?' snorted Barcus, looking around at his tribe and shaking his big head. 'Denying his own identity, when it's plain for all to smell! Well, ratty, you will be given one chance of survival – you will fight our heavyweight champion in a grand gladiatorial contest.'

'Fight?' I squeaked, sounding *just* like a rat.

'That's right, A FIGHT TO THE DEATH!' bellowed Barcus and the chamber rang with badger cheers.

'No, you don't understand,' I cried.

'No, bald rat, *you* don't understand. You've got no choice in the matter. Sentence has been passed!' said the badgers' leader.

'So, which one is your champion gladiator?' I asked nervously, looking around the room.

'That would be me,' chuckled Barcus, with a wicked grin.

Goodbye, Cruel World!

I'm now in a little ante-chamber, preparing myself for the coming fight with Barcus, and taking what might be the last opportunity to write up my journal.

Hanging from a hook on the wall is a copper armoured breastplate for me to wear, and a circular metal shield. I have Captain Cut-throat's cutlass for a weapon and I'm pretty good with that, but I'm not kidding myself. I don't stand a chance against Barcus!

Although he only comes up to my shoulder, he is built like a boxer, with great muscle-bound arms, a mouth full of wicked fangs and a ferocious temper! How on earth did I manage to get myself in this deadly situation? Just one swipe with his razor claws would shred me like a piece of cheese in a grater. Oh, help!

My armour

Someone has just knocked on the door, announcing there's five minutes until 'show time'. I'd better get myself ready. If the next page is blank . . . you'll know my terrible fate.

I'm now in a little anti-chamber preparing
myself for the coming fight with the king, and
asking what role... that I'm doing, for
write on my journal...

Hanging from a hook on the wall is a copper
armoured breastplate for me to wear, and a
circular... shield... into One-three's
cutlass... wrapped with
a... he... I see a
...

...shoulder, he is built...
...with great muscle...
...opens a mouth... and
...red fangs...

...to get... in this
...nation. Just one swipe with his claw
would shred me like a piece of cheese in a
... Oh, help.'

...someone has just knocked on the
announcing there's five minutes until my
time. 'I'd better get myself ready. If I... and I
page is blank...' you'll know my terrible fate

The Gladiator Contest

Sorry about the blank page – I wasn't going to write on that horrible stain! How come I'm still here? Let me explain.

An old, greying badger came to collect me. I donned my armour, put on my rucksack and followed him out of the room, down a short passage and into the chamber. Seats had been put out all around the walls and the place was full of noisy badgers. They were chatting excitedly, buying turnip crisps and real bug humbugs from vendors, and generally getting ready for a really fun time!

As I stood by the wall, a wiry badger wearing a sash around his shoulders walked into the centre of the room and held up his paws for silence. When the noise had died down, the referee began his announcement.

'Boars and sows and all our little cubs, welcome to the grand gladiatorial games!' he began, and the crowd erupted in a mighty cheer. My tummy flipped and my knees started to shake.

'Today we are in for a special treat as our leader and champion takes on a snivelling, no good, low-down, cheating opponent!' the ref continued.

'That's you,' muttered the old badger at my side. 'I don't give you five seconds!'

'Introducing in the loser's, I mean the red corner, the challenger – Bald Rat!'

The crowd hissed and booed as my minder pushed me forward. I walked to the centre of the chamber on legs like jelly and stood shivering by the referee.

'And in the blue corner, the champ; our beloved leader, undefeated in six thousand bouts, Barcus Badgerius!' Barcus entered the ring from a side door, clasping his hands together and waving them above his head. The crowd went mad as he stood by my side, shadowboxing and doing a fast foot shuffle.

'Oi'm gonna bash you! Oi'm gonna crush you! Oi'm gonna tear you limb from limb,' he roared. 'A straight jab to the jaw, a swift uppercut, then a *rip* with my claws and it'll all be over! I am the greatest. Yeah!'

The crowd cheered again, whooping and stomping on the ground. 'BarCUS! BarCUS! BarCUS!'

He wasn't wearing any armour and the only weapon he carried was his big wooden club, but I still didn't rate my chances. I wasn't going to let him know how scared I was, though.

'So, what happens when I win?' I asked. 'Will I be set free?'

'Gnarr!' roared the champ, spraying spit into my face and curling back his lips to show a line of terrible teeth. 'You won't win, Bald Rat! There's only ever one winner and that be me. Oi am Barcus Badgerius, Commander of the Armies of the Badgers, General of the Animal Legions, and true Emperor of the Forest. Oi will have my vengeance, against all invadin' rats. Aarg!'

'Yeah, whatever,' I replied. 'So what are the rules?'

'Rules? There's only one rule, you bumpkin. The winner lives, and the loser . . .' and here, Barcus drew his finger slowly across his throat. 'Got it?'

'Er, got it,' I said. Oh help!

'Right,' said the referee. 'I want a good,

clean fight with plenty of scratchin', bitin' and gougin'. May the best badger win! Go to your corners, gladiators. Let's get ready to rumble!'

'Fight, fight, fight,' roared the crowd as we retired to our corners. Then, *clang!* a bell rang and as a hundred butterflies flittered inside my tummy, the gladiatorial contest began.

Boy Versus Badger!

The crowd stopped cheering and started stamping on the ground in a slow, menacing rhythm that echoed all around the chamber. Then Barcus charged at me, swinging the club above his head.

He was on me before I realized what was happening and I only just managed to raise my shield. *Crash!* The club smashed against the metal sending judders right up my arm and knocking me to the ground. The badger roared and swung his club again, bringing it whipping towards my head, as I lay prone in the dust. *Thump!* I rolled out of the way as the cudgel hit the ground, missing me by centimetres!

'Grrr!' Barcus growled in disappointment

and came marching towards me as I scrambled
to my feet. Now I was expecting him and as he
charged forwards I parried with my cutlass, and
the badger had to dodge out of the way to avoid

its sharp point. We circled each other to the sound of the stamping crowd.

I didn't want to hurt this badger, but I was in a sticky situation and I could tell he wasn't taking any prisoners, so I attacked. I lunged with the cutlass, trying to flick the bludgeon from Barcus's grip. He swept it aside with ease and brought the club swinging down over his head. Again I raised the shield and again it shuddered as the weapon bashed against it. Then, using it like a battering ram, he slammed it into my stomach.

'Aargh!' I went flying backwards, sprawling on the ground, dazed and winded. My armoured breastplate was crumpled in the middle and without it I would surely have been finished. With a terrible grin, the badger came at me like an express train. I raised my sword and he stuttered to a halt, the point only centimetres away from his hairy chest. But, using all his might, he swung the cudgel sideways. With a crack my only weapon was smashed in two. Yikes! I grabbed a piece, now no bigger than a dagger, and ran from my one-eyed adversary.

The crowd went mad as they sensed blood. I retreated across the square, fumbling in the

My sword was smashed in two Yikes!

rucksack that I still wore on my back. I grabbed my water bottle – that was no good. I seized a bat skull – useless. My fingers closed around my lasso. Ah, that was better! Thank goodness I'd brought it with me from the treehouse. I pulled the lariat from the rucksack and looped it over my shoulder.

Barcus was a little more wary now he realized the battle wasn't going to be as straightforward as he'd thought. He paced forward, his good eye flitting from the broken cutlass to the lasso, passing his club from one paw to the other.

'Fight, fight, fight!' roared the crowd, standing up all around the room.

'You're pretty good,' panted Barcus a little out of breath.

'You're not so bad yourself,' I gasped as we circled each other again.

'Aye, we could have made a good team, you 'n' me, if you weren't vermin,' he grunted. 'Pity it 'as to end loik this.' With that, the badger charged again. I unfurled my lasso, span it around my head and let it go. I only had this one chance or I would be battered to paste. Barcus raised the cudgel in one paw and swished the claws of his other as he rumbled forwards with a determined look on his face.

The lasso sailed through the air and fell over his shoulders. I pulled hard to tighten the noose and the badger stopped in his tracks, staring down at the rope in surprise.

'Got you!' I cried, but I spoke too soon. Barcus grabbed the lasso in his powerful paw and yanked with all his might. The other end was still wrapped around my shoulder for anchorage and the violent tug whipped me off my feet and I fell with a crump onto my backside.

'I don't think so, baldy,' growled the badger and charged again.

Oh heck, what could I do now? Reaching into my rucksack with shaking hands I grabbed the

first thing my fingers closed around. Oh flippin'
heck, it was the bat skull again. What could I do
with that? Then, as the monster badger towered
over me, I had an idea. I pulled the two sections
of the jaw apart and threw them
under Barcus's feet. His big
back paw came down on
the upturned bat skull.

'*Yeeow!*' cried the
badger as the sharp bat
fangs pierced the soft pad
of his foot. He hopped up
and down, nursing the injured
paw. But then his good foot
landed on the other half of the skull! 'Double
yeeow!' cried Barcus. He crashed to the floor
like a felled tree and bashed his head on the
ground.

'Gnarr!' he gasped. The wind had been
knocked right out of him and the bump to the
head had left him completely confused. I raced
forward and placed the point of the broken
cutlass against his chest, kneeling on his arms
to prevent him using his deadly claws. There
was no strength left in him for the moment
and looking at me with one confused eye, he

muttered, 'You did it, rat. You've got me. Now finish the job.'

The crowd went silent. I looked over at the referee. Hesitatingly, he extended his arm and slowly turned his thumb to the floor. I knew what that meant. Destroy him! But looking down at Barcus, I knew I couldn't do it. I know he seemed slightly unhinged, but who wouldn't be if an invading army of rats had routed them from their ancestral home? No, it wasn't right.

I got to my feet and holding up the remains of my sword, dropped it to the ground. 'No!' I shouted to the crowd of silent badgers. 'There'll be no killing today.'

'You've got to,' said Barcus from the floor. 'It's the rule – the only rule there is!'

'Well I'm not going to,' I said. 'I've got no quarrel with you.'

Barcus looked confused as he got gingerly to his feet. 'Maybe you're not a rat after all,' he said. 'A rat would *never* spare a badger's loif.'

'I've told you time and time again I am *not* a rat, I am a human being, washed up on this god-forsaken headland! I was attacked by the fetid rats myself. If my friend Knee-high was here, he would tell you,' I cried.

And just then I heard a high pitched 'Peep!' and everyone turned around to see a nervous-looking little mole scuttling into the sett. My faithful friend had managed to track me down!

Making Plans

Knee-high, Barcus, a couple of his generals and I were all sitting around a table in Barcus's private den. It was a richly-furnished room, with deep, patterned carpets on the floor and fine tapestries on the wall, depicting scenes from badger history. In one corner was a big, four-poster bed, and one wall was lined with shelves of books. Near to our table was a writing desk with papers strewn about in a haphazard fashion.

'Peep, peep, peep,' Mole was saying to Barcus.

'Is that so? Well Oi never,' said the badger. 'Did you get that?' he asked me.

Peep

'I'm afraid I don't speak mole,' I said.

'Sorry, Oi thought because you spoke such good badger, you might speak mole as well.'

'But I can't speak badger,' I said. 'Whatever gave you that impression?'

'Because you're speakin' it now,' said Barcus, looking surprised.

'No, I'm speaking human,' I said.

'Sounds just loik badger to me,' said the badger. ''Ow strange. Maybe you yumans, or whatever you call yourself, picked it up from us badgers. That would explain it.'

'Or you badgers picked it up from us yumans,' I said.

'Well,' said Barcus looking around the room at his fellow badgers and chuckling. 'That's 'ardly likely, is it? Anyway, what your peeping pal 'ere was sayin' backs up your story entirely. You did fight the rats, and saw 'em off too! You also helped moley when he was lost and gave 'im an 'ome. Oi think we owe you an apology, Charlie Small.'

'There's no need,' I said. 'We all make mistakes. Even badgers' noses!'

'Yes, well you might be right there,' coughed the badger, a little embarrassed. 'But what Oi can't understand is, if you're not a hairless sort of rat, why is there one just like you living at the rats' village?'

'Another like me – what do you mean?'

'Just that. Living with the stinking rats is a bald-skinned creature just like you. Only bigger. With not as much hair on 'is head.'

'It must be a man,' I cried. 'What's a man doing mixed up with the likes of those vicious vermin?'

'I've no idea,' said Barcus. 'Perhaps we ought to find out.'

'Perhaps we should,' I agreed.

A Recce At Rat Village

After a supper of tough and muddy root vegetables, Knee-high and I stayed the night at the badgers' sett. In the morning Barcus and I sneaked off through the forest to spy on the Rat Village. On the way he told me about the rapacious rat invaders.

'They attacked us in the night, taking us by surprise,' Barcus explained, as the two of us carefully made our way along the badgers' secret tracks through the forest.

'We have no idea where they came from, but there were hundreds of the devils. They invaded the forest like a stinkin' plague. If we'd been ready, the blighters wouldn't have found it so easy. They took prisoners and sacrificed some of our finest warriors on a big stone slab. Of course, as soon as the weasels saw which way the wind was blowin', they joined the enemy. But they're no threat on their own.'

'What did you do next?' I asked.

'There was only one thing Oi could do. Oi led what was left of my people away from our ancient setts and, in the most secret part of the forest, set up a new 'ome. We've been planning a counter-attack for some time now, but Oi'm not sure we're strong enough yet.'

'Are the rats still looking for you?' I asked.

'Oh, they're always searchin'. You were prob'ly attacked by one of the patrols out lookin' for us. Oi hate 'em, Charlie. They've killed so many, so needlessly.'

'It sounds dreadful,' I said, shaking my head.

'Before the invasion, all the animals of the forest lived in harmony – in balance as it were, but they've bin driven away. The rats 'ave taken over the woodland and dumped all their rubbish in our biggest water supply, poisonin' the pond and turnin' it into a toxic chemical soup. They're killin' the forest, that's what they're doin', Charlie!'

I felt so sorry for the forest animals and wished I could do something to help. But what can one boy do against a village of giant rats?

After ages tramping through the forest, Barcus sniffed the air and said, 'We're getting close now, Charlie. Don't make a sound. There'll be lookouts all over the place.'

I followed the badger as he crawled into a long, prickly bank of bushes. We pushed through the branches as quietly as we could.

We were getting close

All of a sudden I heard a noise and a wave of the familiar nauseous smell filled my nose. As I lay hidden in the brush a pair of rat's scabby feet stopped right by my face and was soon joined by another. They started squeaking and chattering to each other as I held my breath until, eventually, they moved away.

We carried on, crawling over the ground like
commandos, until all of a sudden there was the
village before us. The sour smell of rat saturated
the air as I peered out from my hiding place.

The giant rodents had cut down trees and
burnt off the ground cover, creating a wide,
open space about the size of a football pitch.
Small mud huts, roughly thatched with fern
leaves, had been built all around the area and
on top of each miserable hut was a gleaming
white skull. Ugh! I thought. What creepy cretins
they are. Close by, almost filling one end of the
open square was a much larger hut with a deep
overhanging roof, a wide verandah running
all the way around and walls made entirely of
victims' remains.

Part of Rat Village

'When they've done away with their prisoners, they throw 'em into the toxic pond,' explained Barcus in a whisper. 'The poisonous water strips the skeleton of flesh and they fish out the bare skulls for their war trophies.'

I shuddered in repulsion and vowed I must never be taken prisoner by the giant rats. I didn't want to end up as a brick in someone's kitchen extension!

Leader's hut ➚

In the porch of the skull hut was a chair and table where someone had recently been having a meal, for it was littered with gnawed bones and the discarded skins of exotic fruits. This hut had been built with much more care than the rest of the hovels and it didn't take a genius to work out that it was the home of the rat supremo.

King Rat

As we watched, some rats hurriedly appeared from behind one of the smaller buildings and scurried over to where three hollow tree stumps lay on the far side of the square. Taking two long bleached thighbones in each hand, they started thumping out a slow menacing beat.

Rats and weasels started to pour out of the huts. Squealing and snapping at each other bad-temperedly, they gathered in the centre of the square. Soon the area was heaving with fetid rodents, but I didn't see any sign of the human that Barcus said lived in the village.

'Something's about to 'appen,' whispered Barcus.

As the banging of the drums reached a crescendo, making the air seem to vibrate with their powerful thumping, the door to the skull hut crashed open and a figure emerged onto the verandah. It was the Rat King! He was even taller than the others, almost as big as Barcus, and was immensely fat, with double chins rippling down to his hairy chest. He held a ceremonial mace in one hand and a lopsided crown sat on his broad head.

'Meep!' he began, lifting the mace in the air, and the crowd fell silent. 'Meep, neep pip squeak eek!' And for the next quarter of an hour he gave a rousing speech to his enthralled audience. I didn't understand a word but Barcus, who was fluent in rat, translated for me.

King Rat

'He sez it's time to rid the forest of badgers once and for all,' Barcus whispered. 'They know we're in hidin' somewhere and now they're closer to findin' our lair than ever before. Just yesterday mornin', he sez, his spies followed a mole and a boy as they rampaged through the forest on the back of a roarin' monster.'

'Oh no! We've given away your hiding place,' I said, feeling rotten.

'Never mind,' said Barcus, listening to the speech. 'They still 'aven't found it. They got lost along the secret paths. But the king is sendin' out his weasel force tomorrow. They're expert trackers and it's only a matter of time before they find us. In the meantime the rats are goin' to build up their armoury for the mother of all battles, and then they'll wipe my clan from the forest for good.' As Barcus listened to the speech he became angrier and angrier. 'Grrr! The vile vermin, Oi'll show 'em.' And he got up in a fury, about to rush into the arena.

'No, Barcus, you won't stand a chance!' I said in a loud whisper. 'You can't do anything now.'

'Oi've got to do somethin', Charlie,' he said, reluctantly lying down again. 'As soon as they discover our 'ideout, they're gonna attack us.

We're still not strong enough to take on these rebellious rodents and it will mean the end of the badgers and the 'ole forest. Once they've laid waste to it, they'll move on somewhere else.'

I didn't know what to say, and wondered if I should stick around and try to help the beleaguered beasts. But what difference could I make? I was only one small eight-year-old boy, even if I had been around for four hundred years! Then I remembered the Armoured Armadillo. *That* might make some sort of difference.

The fat Rat King finished his speech and sank into his chair. As the crowd dispersed, the monarch squealed loudly towards his hut and when I saw who came out into the arena, I knew I would *have* to fight the rats whether I wanted to or not!

A Terrible Shock!

The door to the king's hut opened in response to his call, and from the dark interior, a man hobbled out.

'That's 'im, that's the creature Oi told you

about. The one that looks just like you,' said Barcus, nudging me.

'You're right,' I said. 'It is a man. But why is he walking so funnily?'

The man was carrying a tray piled with food, limping along in short, stuttering strides. He was bent forwards so I couldn't see his face, but there was something about him that was very familiar. Was it someone I'd already met on my adventures, someone from Destiny Mountain or the Underworld perhaps?

Looking down at his ankles, I saw he was wearing heavy manacles. That's why he's walking so awkwardly, I thought to myself. 'He's a prisoner!' I whispered. 'Look, he's in chains.'

'You're right,' said Barcus. 'And I thought he was one of them. Poor devil, Oi wouldn't want to be a slave to that motley crew. His life must be an absolute misery.'

The man placed the tray on the table next to the Rat King and bowed even lower.

'Meep, eek!' screeched the king and, picking up a fly-swat, rapped him on the head with the handle. The man backed away and stood up slowly. Now I could see him properly as a look of fury flashed across his face.

'NO!' I gasped out loud and for just a second, my heart stopped beating.

'Shhh! You'll have the rat 'oards on us in a minute. What's the matter?' said Barcus.

'I know him!' I cried. 'I know that man – *it's my dad!*'

A look of anger flashed across the man's face – Yikes! it was my dad

Back At The Sett

I was in such a state of shock I have no idea how I got back to the badgers' sett. What on earth could my dad be doing here? I'd been trying to get back home to Mum and Dad for four hundred years and now he had turned up as a slave to a gang of vile and vicious vermin in this dank and dingy forest! What the heck was going on?

I didn't know what to think. But it was so fantastic to see him again! I couldn't wait to find out all about his adventures, and I knew immediately what I must do. I would have to fix the Armoured Armadillo, help the stricken badgers in their war against the rats and FREE MY DAD FROM SLAVERY!

'Of course we'll help,' said Barcus as we sat at the table in his den. We were holding a council of war with the badger generals, making plans to pre-empt the rats and strike at them before they had a chance to attack us. 'We 'aven't got much time, though,' he continued. 'It won't be long before the weasel scouts track down this sett, and then they'll strike with all their might.'

'If we can fix the Armadillo, I think it could

I've got to save dad!!!

give us an edge,' I said, excitedly. 'Jakeman's inventions usually have a secret trick or two hidden somewhere. If not, at least we can use it as a tank to burst through the forest into their village and bash a few rats with its thumping great tail. It will scare the pants off them!'

''Ow long do you think it will take?' asked Barcus.

'Two or three days,' I said.

'Ooh,' said Barcus taking a deep breath. 'That's cutting it mighty fine, Charlie. Still, it's our only chance. We'll get started first thing in the mornin'. Agreed?'

'Agreed,' the generals responded.

'Peep,' said Knee-high.

Preparing For War

I've been working flat out for two days and this is the last entry in my journal before the big bash. This evening I'm going with the badger army to make a surprise attack on the Rat Village. Oh, yikes!

I stayed the night with the badgers again, sleeping on a mattress of warm, dry straw, full up from a hearty dinner of woodland grubs and insects. They didn't taste too bad, a bit like crispy snacks. The only ones I didn't like were some big, fat maggoty-looking things that were full of custardy juice and burst in your mouth when you bit them.

Yuk!

In the morning, the badgers loaded the crashed Armadillo onto a long, heavy cart and pulled it deep into the undergrowth, covering their tracks behind them. Then I set to work.

I bashed out some dents in the armour with one of the badger's clubs and fixed a damaged joint in the Armadillo's neck. Now the head could move freely, like an oscillating battering ram! Discovering the machine's eyes could be made to flash, I reconnected some loose wiring. I also found out what the Armadillo's secret weapon was – and how to use it!

oops! I spilt some oil

A chubby, matronly badger called Bathsheba gave me a hand, and Knee-high was a great help. He patiently passed spanners and screwdrivers, fetching this and that and supplying us with endless mugs of herb tea. At one point, a badger lookout hissed a warning. 'Sssh! Everyone down tools.'

We stopped work and held our breath as a rat patrol passed by, only a few metres from our camp. Eventually we were given the all-clear and I carried on, but it was a timely reminder of just how close the enemy was getting.

The next day I finished all the repairs, oiled the joints, checked all the levels and gave the machine a good polish until it glinted and gleamed like a new car. I was just in time, for at midday Barcus called an emergency meeting.

'Oi've got some important news,' said Barcus, bringing out a map of the Rat Village. 'Oi sent a member of the SBS, the Special Badger Service, to check out Rat Village this mornin'. She's just reported back that the rodents are havin' a big meetin' tonight – it'll be the King's final briefin' to his troops. She reckons they know where our sett is and plan to launch an attack at dawn tomorrow.'

'Jeepers!' I said.

'Aye, jeepers indeed, young Charlie; we're only just ready in time and we have no choice but to attack *tonight*. This is what we'll do . . .'

Barcus and his generals explained that we would split into two groups and attack the village in a pincer movement. Waiting until the rat meeting was in full swing, we would strike from opposite ends of the square, trapping the rats in the middle. I would drive the Armadillo around, scaring the enemy witless and causing as much mayhem as possible. Here is the actual map that Barcus used to plan the attack:

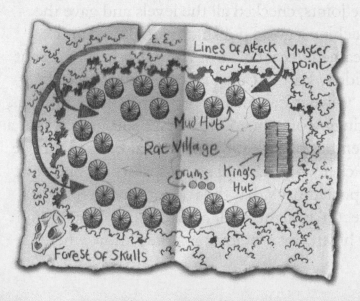

It seems like a good strategy. I only hope the Armoured Armadillo starts! Wish me luck!

Taking Up Position

We couldn't risk driving the noisy Armadillo to Rat Village as it would alert the enemy of our approach, so we loaded it onto the badger's cart and, as quietly as possible, dragged it through the forest.

At first we made such a noise of cracking branches that Barcus sent a few of his men on ahead to silently clear the ground in advance of the cart. It was a slow process, but with the added protection of wrapping the cartwheels in sacking, we made steady progress.

An amazing thing happened as we trudged through the forest. Woodland animals started to appear from the undergrowth and joined the line behind us! There were wily foxes and a strong-looking otter; a lone wild boar; a few boxing-mad hares and even one magnificent stag with huge spreading antlers.

Barcus grinned. 'They're all startin' to come 'ome,' he said. 'Oh, we mustn't fail 'em now!'

As we neared Rat Village, Barcus spied a couple of sentries through the foliage, and signalled for us to stop. Taking a spare sack from the pile we'd used to dampen the noise of the cartwheels, Barcus gestured to me to follow Bella, a member of his famous SBS troop (there were only two members of the SBS, and Barcus himself was the other one!). We crawled on our hands and knees into the thicket, Bella directing me where to go with complicated hand signals. Circling around the rat sentries as quietly as mice, we crept up behind them. Bella pointed at one of the sentries and then at me. We crept closer to our quarry and I waited, crouched on the ground, watching for a signal. The badger held up a fist and then, one after the other, raised three clawed fingers. One, two, three, GO!

I jumped up and in one fluid movement dropped the sack over the rat's head, Then, drawing the ball of string from my rucksack, I wound it round and round the animal until he was tied as tight as a parcel. At the same time,

Bella had clamped her big paw around the other rat's mouth and wrestled him to the ground. I threw the remains of my ball of string to her and she tied up the other sentry. Brilliant – job done and no noise made. I was getting quite good at this commando stuff!

As the thudding drums signalling the start of the rat's meeting began, Bella let out a low whistle, and the rest of the troops shuffled forward. With a mighty heave six burly badgers lifted the Armadillo from the cart. Their paws slipped, and the monstrous machine crashed to the ground, shaking the bushes all around us.

'Shhh!' whispered Barcus, agitated. 'You're makin' enough noise to wake the dead!' But the drums continued thumping and now we heard the piping squealing voice of the King starting his speech.

'Right, it's time. Everyone take up your positions!'

I gulped – this was it! I was about to go into battle against an army of highly trained rats and their weaselly cohorts. I was beginning to wish I was safely back at the sett with Knee-high and the cubs.

The Deciding Battle

As the badgers lined up just inside the line of trees that surrounded the open square of Rat Village, I climbed into the driving seat of the Armoured Armadillo. I checked the controls and flipped down a flap in the fascia that revealed a row of buttons that controlled the machine's secret weapon. This, I hoped, would help us defeat our impressive foe. If it worked, that is – I'd had no opportunity to test it!

Through the leaves of the overhanging trees, I could make out the Rat King. He was standing on a raised platform by the side of his skull hut and was in full flow, squeaking and gesticulating wildly. Every now and then he paused impressively, striking a heroic pose, and the crowd of heavily armed rats and weasels burst into loud applause. I couldn't see any sign of Dad, though.

Then with a mighty growl, Barcus led his troops into battle. They rushed out into the open, thumping their clubs on the ground and pulling their muzzles back in terrible snarls to show their long, vicious fangs. For a moment the crowd of rats froze in astonishment. Their king carried on with his squeaking speech, oblivious to what was going on behind him. Then he realized something was up and span around.

'*Sssss,*' he hissed when he saw the charging badgers. 'MEEP!' he screamed, and immediately the commander of the rat troops led a battalion of rodents to meet them. At the same time, the rest of the badgers, the foxes and hares and the mighty stag burst from the trees at the other end of the square and came charging

CHARGE!

and hollering across the ground.

Within seconds it was complete chaos. Badgers and rats were locked in mortal combat. Weasels and hares were knocking seven bells out of each other; the stag tossed rats into the air with his antlers – and now it was time for *me* to act.

I grabbed the starter handle and pulled. Just like before, nothing happened.

'Don't fail me now,' I cried, but no matter how many times I pulled the handle the machine refused to start. It didn't even give a polite cough. What was wrong with the flaming thing? Had the crash completely ruined the engine?

Then I remembered! Oh, what a fool. When I'd been mending the machine I'd turned off the petrol feed pipe for safety. I scrambled across the Armadillo's back and lifted the engine hood. I plunged my hand down between the tubes and spark plugs and drive belts, feeling around for the fuel tap. Ah! There it was. I gave it a turn, slammed the hood shut and dived back into my seat. I pulled the starter handle again and the engine roared into life, as throaty as a sports car.

'Yee-hah!' I cried and thrust the levers forward, pumping the accelerator pedal with my foot. The Armadillo leaped forward and went careering through the trees. We burst out of the forest, bringing down a cascade of leaves and branches and went lumbering towards the square like a manic tortoise.

I turned the eyes on and they flashed menacingly. I pumped the throttle again and the exhaust roared like a lion. A group of rats stared in horror and froze, their mouths hanging open. With a quick biff-baff, a large badger bashed them on the bonce with his club and they crumpled to the ground. When another pack of weasels saw the advancing machine, they dropped their weapons and ran for the forest, wriggling and writhing in fear.

'*Yahoo!*' I screamed. 'Come and get some if you think you're hard enough!'

There were still plenty of rats left, though.

Lots more than there were of us in fact, and the battle raged on.

Boy Versus Rat!

I steered the Armoured Armadillo through the crowd of battling animals straight towards the mud huts. As I came alongside the first row I turned on the tail. It started to swish back and forth and caught the wall of the first hut a crushing blow with its mighty mace. *Crash!* The dried mud wall of the hut shattered like glass and crumbled to the ground, bringing the thatched roof with it. I moved onto the next hut and then the next one, leaving the rat's homes in a pile of rubble.

BASH!

Just then one of the few remaining weasels leaped onto the back of my machine, lifted the lid of the engine and thrust his paw inside. He gave a tug and held up one of the spark plugs in triumph. The Armadillo's engine spluttered, misfired and stopped.

'Give it back, you measly weasel,' I demanded, but the creature just chattered in delight and threw the spark plug down to the rat commander. He gave an evil sneer and squealed as if to say, 'if you want it, come and get it.'

I had no choice; I had to get that spark plug back. I slid down from my seat and the commander came towards me, drawing a thin foil from his belt.

'Meep eep,' he sneered.

'Meep eep to you too,' I replied, bending down to pick up a long piece of wood, a thin beam from the roof of one of the demolished huts. I could use it as a quarterstaff, like Little John in the Robin Hood stories.

The commander thrust with his foil and I span my staff and blocked it, knocking it away. He lunged again, twirling the point in the air and trying to catch my fingers. I managed to sidestep the attack and brought the beam crashing down on top of his thick skull.

'*Eeek,*' he leered in anger. He threw the spark plug to his weasely pal and I leaped in the air to try and catch it. I missed; the weasel grabbed it and waved it in my face, taunting me and chattering in excitement. I rushed at him, but the animal threw the plug back to the commander and for the next few minutes we played a game of piggy in the middle, the two bullying animals throwing the vital engine part back and forth between them.

'Give it back, you vermin,' I yelled, but try as I might, I just couldn't retrieve it.

Tiring of the game, the commander made a head-on rushing assault. I span the quarterstaff, smacking his sword, bending the end and cracking him behind the ear. Immediately I twisted around,

sweeping the staff along the ground in a wide arc and caught the weasel a blow on his ankles.

'*Ssss!*' he hissed, crashing to the ground and dropping the plug. I dived on it, thrust it in my pocket and, doing a quick roll, jumped to my feet and faced the commander. He was charging right at me, his bent foil swishing in the air. I bashed it out of the way, turned my staff and caught him with the end, right in the stomach.

'Oof!' the commander cried, dropping to his knees and fighting for breath.

I ran to the Armadillo and, fumbling with nerves, plugged the crucial plug back in place. I was only just in time, for as I clambered back in my seat the rat had already got his breath back and was struggling to his feet. *Brrrm!* The engine kicked into life and as the rat tried to jump onto the back of the Armadillo, I turned the tail on. The heavy mace swung around, catching the rat full on his side and sending him sailing high into the air to land deep in the undergrowth. Phew! That was a close one.

Saving Dad!

I pushed the levers forward and the machine marched on, demolishing huts as we went and leaving them in clouds of swirling mud dust.

All around, the battle was raging as furiously as ever. Most of the weasels had disappeared; things had become too hot for them and they escaped into the forest, screaming their high-pitched squeals. A few had even decided that they were on a losing ticket and changed sides, fighting alongside the badgers against their former rat masters. Barcus had been right – weasels have got no staying power!

All of a sudden I was marching straight at the Rat King's hut of grisly skulls. Outside the main door a small group of rats were guarding the building. The fat King was probably hiding inside, knees knocking and his roll of chins wobbling like jellies on a plate!

The guards raised their swords. I thrust the levers forward to top speed and turned on the flashing eyes again. When they saw the mechanical monster coming straight towards them, eyes burning and blunt head moving from side to side as if it were sniffing them out, the

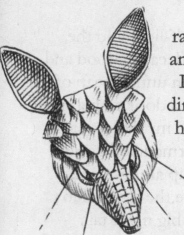

rats dropped their weapons and scarpered.

I drove the Armadillo directly at the front of the hut and with a terrible crash the wall collapsed, skulls dropping like rocks all around me and bouncing and rolling across the ground.

As we ploughed into the main room of the hut I saw an enormous hairy bottom trying to squeeze out of the back window. The Rat King was trying to escape! He was stuck tight but, driven by fear, made one last mighty effort. He shot from the window like a cork from a bottle, tumbled across the ground and lay there screaming for his guard.

Putting the Armadillo in neutral, I looked around the skull hut. It was a bare room, the

← The rat king's fat bottom

white walls glowing in the half-light and the floor littered with scraps of decaying food and rubbish. In one corner was an untidy heap of dirty bedding and in another a door with a small, barred window. That's where my dad must be, I thought, and putting the Armadillo in gear, I drove it forward until I was up alongside it.

'Stand back!' I yelled above the Armadillo's noisy engine, and swung the big mace tail. It smashed into the door, shattering it to matchwood and my dad hobbled cautiously out of his prison, looking completely confused.

'Charlie?' he gasped. 'Charlie? What on earth are you doing here?'

'I might ask you the same question, Dad, but there's no time to explain! Get in the Armadillo!' I said, excitedly. I was so pleased to see him again!

Dad just stood in a daze.

'Quickly, Dad, there's a battle to fight!' I cried.

'Oh, right-ho, Charlie,' he replied, still looking totally bemused. He

tried to climb up into the mechanimal, but the chain hobbling his ankles was very short and he couldn't lift his foot high enough.

'Sit down, Dad,' I said. 'Sit down with your legs stretched out in front.'

Dad obeyed, not having a clue what was going on. As soon as he was in position, I backed up the Armadillo and, lifting the machine's tail, brought the mace thundering down onto the chain. *Ker-ping!!*

'What the . . . ?' cried Dad in petrified astonishment.

'Stay very still, Dad,' I ordered as I repeated the action and the big metal ball of spikes smashed between his ankles.

CRUMP! Two of the links cracked and the chain fell in half.

'Now come on, there's no time to lose!'

Dad climbed into the Armadillo and I turned it around and went rumbling back through the hole in the wall and into the thick of the action. It was time to use the Armadillo's secret weapon!

The Gunge Gun!

'What on earth's going on, Charlie?' asked Dad, still with a look of someone in a dream.

'I'll explain later. Now hold on tight!' The Armoured Armadillo rocked wildly as we climbed over some rubble from the skull hut. Dad looked at me with a worried expression.

'Careful, Charlie – I think you'd better let me drive. You haven't even got a licence!' he said.

'Don't panic, Dad,' I sighed. 'I've been doing this sort of thing for four hundred years!' Scanning the square, I saw that Barcus

1. SMALL
2. CHARLIE
3. 17-04-01   FOREST OF SKULLS
4a. 20-06-09   4b. LICENCE TO DRIVE ARMOURED ARMADILLOS

Charlie Small

ADDRESS: BADGER SETT, FOREST OF SKULLS, BROCKSHIRE BS1 FS

What would an armoured armadillo licence look like?

had cornered the Rat King against the ruined wall of one of the huts. The king's elite guards surrounded their leader and they were just managing to hold Barcus off. Elsewhere, bashing and bopping was still going on all over the village. Rats were sitting around on the ground, dazed from being clumped on the head by the badgers' clubs. Badgers were nursing cuts and bruises from the rats' foils and their germy teeth. All in all it looked about even. But I had the weapon to change all that!

I directed the Armadillo at a large group of fighting animals. 'Out of the way, badgers,' I ordered. 'Retreat!'

The badgers immediately let their clubs drop to their sides and looked at me questioningly. They had no idea what I was about to do, but they obeyed and scurried out of the way. The rats started to cheer, thinking that they had got the upper hand at last. Little did they know!

I opened the flap in the fascia and pressed one of the buttons on the panel underneath. A small hatch opened on the Armadillo's shoulders and a nozzle slid forward.

'What are you doing, Charlie?' asked Dad. 'How come you know how to operate this thing – and what the heck is it, anyway?'

'Later, Dad, later,' I grinned. 'Just sit back and enjoy the ride!'

'Hey rats, say cheese!' I yelled, and as if they were posing for a group photo the rats turned to look at us. Some of them even smiled! I pressed another button and with a *whoosh* the nozzle sent out a powerful jet of bright blue gel. It splattered the rats, covering them from head to toe. Some tried to run for it, but as soon as they were touched by the liquid, they froze in their tracks like a set of statues at a stately home.

'It's a special quick-drying jelly that Jakeman developed,' I explained to Dad.

'Oh, I see,' said Dad. 'Charlie . . .'

'Yes?' I asked, squirting the gun again to freeze more rats in a variety of petrified poses.

'Who the heck is Jakeman?'

'He's a pal of mine, the inventor who made this machine. The jelly sets as hard as concrete in a matter of seconds. There's a little pamphlet in the glove compartment that explains it all.'

'But that's terrible!' Dad exclaimed. 'I know the rats are disgusting, nasty and vindictive vermin but they'll slowly starve to death, covered up like that!'

'Don't worry,' I replied. 'The booklet says the cement wears off after a couple of hours. By then we could have caged the lot, or sliced them into vermicelli!'

'My goodness, Charlie, I had no idea you were so gory!'

'There's a lot you don't know about me, Dad, and this is a matter of life and death!'

The Toxic Pond

When the rats saw their companions being
turned into living statues, they started to panic,
running around in circles and trying to escape
into the forest. I started to herd them up, driving
them towards the badgers. Banging their clubs
on the ground, the badgers turned the flood
of rodents down a wide track that led from the
square.

'Rarr!' the badgers roared in unison and gave
chase. Dad and I followed in the rampaging
Armadillo. I pumped the accelerator, making the
engine growl like a demented dragon. Leading
the fleeing rats was their king, waddling at top
speed and squealing all the way. He tripped and
fell and the stream of rats ran right over him,
trampling him into the dirt. So
much for his loyal subjects!

The king scrambled to his
feet just as Barcus caught
up with him. The badger
swung his big club
and whacked
the rat on his
ample rump,

making him ripple and quiver like a bowl of cold, coagulated custard.

'MEEP!' cried the king and he waddled clumsily away even faster, along the track as it sloped downhill towards another clearing in the trees.

Up ahead, through the overhanging branches, I could see a wide pond, green with algae and scum. It bubbled and popped, sending clouds of steam into the air that spread out to form a thick, swirling blanket of mist.

'Ugh!' Dad exclaimed. 'What's that?'

'It must be the toxic pond,' I said. 'The rats have polluted it and use it to decompose their victims.'

'They do what?' gasped Dad. 'Charlie, what have you got yourself mixed up in?'

I didn't have time to answer; I was using all my concentration trying to keep the Armadillo upright as we careered down the slope to the clearing.

The badgers bashed their clubs on the ground and roared. The stag bellowed and the hares thumped their large feet. Stricken with fear the rats headed straight for the steaming, fetid pond and, like a pack of lemmings, dived right into the toxic soup of bubbling chemicals; all except the king who fell to his knees and with his front paws clasped together, meeped and squeaked for mercy!

Barcus grabbed him by the scruff of the neck and hauled him to his feet.

'Bella,' he called. 'Keep an eye on this creep.'

As Bella led King Rat away, the pond began to sizzle and hiss. Clouds of vapour boiled into the air like steam from a kettle, obscuring the pond from view. The stench was overwhelming and we all collapsed in fits of rasping coughs and splutters. Eventually, the hissing, belching pond quietened down and the air began to clear. There was not a rat to be seen.

'That's it, Charlie, they've gone,' said Barcus. 'The rat invaders 'ave dissolved!'

The animals cheered in a cacophony of roars, grunts, barks and bellows.

'But that's disgusting!' said Dad.

The rat invaders had dissolved in the pond

My Dad The Hero!

'Oh, Dad,' I sighed. 'Those vermin killed loads of innocent badgers and built Rat Village out of their skulls. They showed no mercy at all. What's more, they somehow had you slaving away for their revolting king!'

'Yes, you're right!' said Dad, and with a grim look on his face he ran at the Rat King and gave him a walloping boot on the backside.

'Meep!' wailed the king.

'That's for all the whacks you gave me, you great bullying bag of blubber!' said Dad. 'What's going to happen to him now?' he asked.

'Oh, we'll build a strong cage to keep 'im in,' chuckled Barcus.

'Dad, this is Barcus, leader of the badger clan, true guardians of the forest,' I said and Barcus shook Dad's hand in his powerful paw. Then, turning to Barcus I added, 'The rat statues will be able to move again soon. The gunge only lasts a little while.'

'Yes, Oi was goin' to ask you 'bout that solidifying gunk you used,' said Barcus. 'That was a touch of genius. Well done, Charlie!'

'Don't thank me, it was all Jakeman's doing,' I said.

'Oh, and I forgot to thank you for rescuing me,' said Dad to the badger, shaking his paw again.

'Think nothin' of it, ol' chap. An enemy of the rats is a friend to the badgers!' smiled Barcus. Typical, I thought. How come Barcus gets all the praise?

'Excuse me, what are we going to do with the gunge-covered rats?' I asked, trying to break up their mutual appreciation society.

'We'll put all of 'em in the cage with their king,' said Barcus. 'If they behave 'emselves, we'll treat 'em well. If not, we'll load the cage onto some floatin' logs and send 'em out to sea. What really concerns me is our pond. It used to contain the sweetest water in the forest. Now it's no more than a bath of bubblin' bacteria.'

'Oh, I might be able to help there,' said Dad and he took a small container from his back pocket and rattled it in the air. 'These might do the trick. They're water purifying tablets; I was about to clean our garden pond at home just before I ended up here.' He turned it upside down, emptying about thirty big tablets into the green water. Immediately, they started to fizz, spreading foam over the surface of the pool. Gradually the water began to clear.

'Give them a few hours and it should be all right for drinking again,' Dad said with satisfaction.

'Why, that's bloomin' marvellous. It's nothin' less than magic,' gasped Barcus. 'You've saved our beautiful pond. You didn't tell me your dad was a miracle worker, Charlie. Three cheers for Dad Small, the hero of the hour,' he cried. 'Hip, hip . . .'

'HOORAY FOR DAD SMALL!' everyone cheered, and lifting my rather surprised dad onto their shoulders, four burly badgers carried him along the track and all the way back to Rat Village.

Hold on a minute, I thought to myself as I was left standing all alone by the water's edge, Dad hasn't done anything special! I'm the one that helped drive out the rats. Shouldn't I be the hero of the hour? Charming!

Hip Hip Hooray!

A Victory Feast

By the time the rats had all been caged and put on the cart and we'd trudged back to the badger sett, it was dawn and I was feeling exhausted. The badgers, though, were in no mood for sleeping. They wanted to celebrate, and before long mountains of food and drink had been brought into the main chamber.

I introduced Dad to Knee-high, who ran over to me the minute we arrived back at camp, his teddy dangling from one paw. He peeped and threw his arms around my legs as I ruffled the top of his head.

Dad was mystified. 'Is all this really happening, Charlie?' he asked as he took a mug of steaming twig tea from a badger. 'Or have I gone completely bonkers?'

'Oh, it's happening all right,' I grinned. 'Grab some food and I'll tell you all about my adventures, and you can tell me yours.'

As a group of badgers started playing rustic-looking guitars and others began to dance, Dad and I went and sat in a quiet corner. Knee-high hurried off to join in the reels as I told Dad all about my adventures from start to finish; he stared in mute astonishment through the whole story.

'But you've only been gone from home an hour or so,' he said, cramming his mouth with popcorn mealy grubs.

'Yes, I know. We're in a different time zone now though, Dad. We're in a completely new world,' I explained. 'So, how did you get here?'

'That's the strange thing,' Dad said. 'I'm not entirely sure. I got home from work and Mum said tea would be a little while, so I went to tidy up the garden. I raked out all the leaves from the fish pond and took them over to the compost heap . . .'

'And then what?' I prompted him. 'What happened at the compost heap?'

Dad took a massive bite from a slice of pie on his plate and stared into space, trying to remember. 'Mmm, this is delicious, Charlie. Maybe I can ask the badgers for the recipe. What's in it?'

'Worms!' I said and Dad choked.

'Are you trying to poison me, Charlie?' he spluttered, spitting out a mouthful of half-chewed filling.

Recipe
for Worm Pie

FOR Dad Small from Barcus with thanks

For pastry:
200g flour
100g butter
Pinch of salt

1. Sift the flour and salt into a bowl and rub in the butter until you have a crumbly mixture.

2. Add 2 tablespoons cold water and stir

3. Make mixture into a rough ball

4. Roll out and line an oven proof bowl

For filling:
900g of fresh worms (deceased)
1 onion
1 handful of forest herbs
1 bottle of badger's ale

1. Chop worms and onion and fry in a spot of oil until golden brown

2 Add ale and herbs. Bring to boil and simmer for 30 minutes

3 Pour into pastry lined bowl. Cover with a pastry lid and cook on medium heat for 1 hour

(May cause stomach cramps
and terrible toilet trouble)

'They're perfectly safe, Dad. I've eaten loads of them,' I sighed. 'Now, getting back to the compost heap . . .'

'Oh yes,' he said. 'I remember now. As I threw the leaves onto the compost, my foot slipped and I fell into it head first!'

'That must've smelled nice,' I laughed.

'Mmm, not really,' said Dad, giving me one of his looks. 'But the weird thing was that I didn't stop. I carried on falling. I went right through the centre of the mound and into an opening in the ground. I fell down a shaft and landed with a painful bump at the bottom.'

'You're joking!' I said.

'It's true, Charlie. I was going to climb straight out, thinking I must've fallen into a disused well or something. Then I noticed a tunnel.'

'Go on,' I said. This was getting interesting!

'I followed the tunnel under next door's garden and on and on until I thought I would come up in the middle of town. Now I reckoned I had to be in a disused sewerage pipe. I could hear dirty sewer rats scurrying all around me. You know I hate rats, Charlie, and I had just decided to go back when I saw a light up ahead. I hurried towards it, desperate to get away from the sound of nibbling rodents.'

eak, squeak, squeak, squeak, squeak, squeak, squeak, squeak, squeak

'This is incredible, Dad!' I gasped. I thought these things only happened to me. Maybe it ran in the Small genes!

'You're right, it *is* incredible,' said Dad. 'I thought I must be having a nightmare. The tunnel ended in a beam of light coming from just above my head, and I scrambled up to find myself in the hollow trunk of a massive tree. The shaft of light came from a huge split in the side of the trunk and I gingerly squeezed out and found myself in this forest! I was so glad to get away from the sound of rats I sat down and took a few deep breaths. Imagine my horror when a gang of the biggest-looking varmints burst from the undergrowth – and they had swords in their hands!'

'Tell me about it,' I said. 'The same thing happened to me!'

'Well, that's about it, really. I was taken prisoner, chained up and made to do the bidding of that revolting Rat King. Ooh, I could batter that bullying beast!' said Dad with a massive shudder.

'Never mind, he's safely locked away now,' I said. Then I had the most amazing, incredible and wonderful thought. 'Dad!' I exclaimed. 'Do you know where this hollow tree is?'

'Well, it's somewhere near Rat Village,' said Dad. 'Why?'

'Because if we can find it, we can go home! After four hundred years I will be able to get back in time for tea! Yee-hah!'

Going Home

For the rest of the day, Dad and I partied with the badgers, the hares, the foxes and all the other animals who had helped drive out the swarm of rats. We cheered as Barcus sang old badger folk songs and Bella performed a dance of strange and ancient beauty. Full up from mud cake and the badgers' dark, bitter ale, we eventually crawled away to bed and slept for hours and hours and hours. In the morning, after I'd written up my journal and was still feeling tired and bleary-eyed, Barcus and

Knee-high helped us search the forest for the big hollow tree that might lead back home.

There was a wonderful surprise when we left the badgers' sett. For the first time since I'd arrived in the forest, the air was alive with birdsong. We could hear a woodpecker hammering on a tree in the distance and a squirrel skitted across the ground in front of us. The animals were returning to their homes.

Locating Dad's hollow tree though, wasn't easy. It was like trying to find a needle in a haystack! There are millions of trees in the forest – and thousands of hollow ones. Every now and then Dad would shout, 'Over here! This is the one!' and we'd all rush over and dive inside to find of course it *wasn't* the one.

I began to despair that we would ever find it when *'Peepeepeep!'* cried Knee-high, running full pelt towards an enormous split tree to the north of Rat Village. He dived inside and, reaching the tree a second or two later, we looked about for him. There was no one there!

Peep!

'Knee-high!' I yelled at the top of my voice.

'Peep!' came a little cry at our feet and, brushing away a carpet of dry leaves, we saw a large hole in the ground, half blocked with twigs and forest debris.

'He's found it!' yelled Dad, as Knee-high's long, velvet snout emerged from the hole and he clambered out. 'The furry little chap has found it. Charlie, we can go home!'

We marked the tree with a big white chalk tick and went to collect our things. I took Dad to my treehouse, where I'd left some of my stuff. Dad hated heights and there was a stiff breeze blowing, making the treehouse sway from side to side. Dad grabbed hold of the balcony rail, looking very pale and wobbly.

'How on earth did you manage to live up here?' he asked, looking as though he was going to be sick.

'It's brilliant, Dad,' I said. 'Just look at the amazing view!'

Dad glanced out towards the ocean, seeing the horizon tilt one way and then the other as the tree rocked back and forth.

'I've got to get down from here, Charlie,' he gasped. '*Now!*'

Back at the hollow tree all the badgers were waiting to see us off.

'We can't thank you enough for all the 'elp you've given us, Dad Small,' said Barcus, shaking our hands solemnly.

'It was nothing,' said Dad. There he goes again, I thought. He didn't do anything other than throw a few tablets in the pond!

Then Barcus took me to one side. 'We know how much we owe you, Charlie; we'll be able to return to our ancient setts, thanks to you. All the badgers would like you to accept this as a token of our eternal gratitude,' he said and handed me the King Rat's crown. It was fashioned from rusty tin cans and inlaid with shards of glass and half-chewed pastilles, but was quite beautiful all the same. I knew I would cherish it as a reminder of my fantastic adventures in the Forest of Skulls.

I gave Knee-high a really big hug. He had started blubbing and I knew that if we didn't get going quickly, he would make me cry too.

'Come on, Dad,' I said and sat down at the edge

of the hole inside the tree trunk. 'Cheerio everyone,' I said and pushed myself forward. I dropped down and landed in the tunnel Dad had described. A second later he was standing by my side.

The sounds from the forest were muffled and, soon after we started walking, they disappeared completely. I took the torch from my rucksack and switched it on. My heart was pattering with excitement at the thought of getting home.

'Are you sure you've got enough in that rucksack?' asked Dad.

'Everything I need,' I smiled. 'Come on, Dad, let's hurry; I can't believe I'm nearly home. And I'm hungry.'

'Me too,' said Dad. 'I wonder what Mum has cooked for tea!'

Home, At Last!

As we jogged along, a curious thing started to happen. The tunnel began to close up behind us, as if a huge force were squashing the earth together like plasticine. There was no way back to the forest and the rapidly closing passage hurried us along until, eventually, we came to the other end and found ourselves at the bottom of a deep shaft. A small circle of light glowed at the top.

'I don't know how we're going to climb up the well, Charlie,' said Dad. 'The sides are pretty sheer.'

'No problem,' I said, taking the lasso from my rucksack. 'Stand back, Dad!'

I whipped the lariat around my head and let it go. It whistled through the air, closing around a large lump of stone sticking out from the wall near the top of the shaft. I gave it a yank to test its strength and then handed the end to Dad.

'After you,' I said. I was feeling very excited. After four hundred years I was nearly home! What's more, Dad knew all about my amazing escapades. He'd seen how I helped drive out a plague of rats; I'd even helped save him from a life of slavery. I chuckled to myself. He'll never be able to tell me off again, I thought. What fun!

Dad climbed the rope and clambered out through the hole at the top. I quickly followed and was soon pulling myself from the middle of the smelly compost heap into my own back garden! There was my house and my very own bedroom window – and there was Mum by the kitchen door. I was so pleased to see her!

'About time too,' she called, drying her hands on a tea towel. 'Tea's nearly ready so come and wash your hands, the pair of you.' It was as though I'd never been away!

I bent down and gathered up my lasso, hooking it over my shoulder. Wow! The opening to the shaft had completely closed behind us and I looked over at Dad to tell him. He was standing with his back to me, gazing up in the sky and scratching the top of his balding head.

'Dad . . .' I began. He turned around. He had the same confused look on his face as when I met him in the King Rat's hut.

'Yes, Charlie?' he asked.

'The hole has gone,' I said. 'The hole to the forest!'

'What hole? What forest? What are you talking about?' he said, looking bemused.

I looked into his eyes and suddenly I realized: he couldn't remember a thing about our adventures!

Yippee, I'm home

What hole?

'It's ok, nothing, Dad,' I said, feeling a bit sad.

'Good lad, run along now; I'll be there in a tick. I just want to finish tidying this compost. It seems to be in a worse state than when I started!' he said, turning back. Ah well. Things were definitely back to normal!

Here We Go Again! Yikes!

I ran into the kitchen where Mum was just putting something on the cooker to boil.

'I'm back, Mum!' I cried, giving her a huge bear hug. It was so good to be home after so long.

'So I see,' said Mum with a grin on her face. 'Oh Charlie, just look at the state of you. Where on earth have you been?'

'Oh, you'll never believe it, Mum. I've been fighting monsters; flying on giant owls; defeating brigands and rats and robbing banks. All sorts!'

'It looks like it, too,' said Mum. 'And did you pick up that carton of milk I asked you to get?'

'Uh? Oh, darn it. I'll go and get it now.'

'You can go and get changed first. You look

as if you've been dragged through a hedge backwards!'

'OK, Mum,' I said. Squeezing past her I grabbed a couple of rock cakes cooling on a tray on the worktop, and rushed upstairs. Stuffing a delicious, warm, buttery cake in my mouth, I opened my bedroom door.

Mmm! One of Mum's rock cakes.

It felt strange to be back home after such a long time. I expected things to have changed, but everything was just the same. My computer, my games and books were all exactly as I'd left them. Then, looking at my super-hero calendar on the wall I realized it was Monday tomorrow. Oh, flip – school! I wasn't sure I was ready to go back to school. Sure, I'd had a four-hundred-year holiday, but it didn't seem quite long enough! Oh well, there wasn't much I could do about that. Had I done my homework? I couldn't remember.

It was brilliant to be back home – and sort of disappointing too. I was going to miss all the friends I'd made in the strange world of adventure. I wondered what Jakeman and Philly were up to? How were all my mates down in the Underworld and did the Perfumed Pirates ever make it to dry land? Oh well, I thought, I suppose I'll never know now.

Pulling on a clean pair of jeans and a new top and dragging my tatty rucksack onto my back, I slid down the banisters into the hall. As soon as I'd got the milk I could sit down to one of Mum's terrific teas! I hoped she hadn't cooked worm pie – I'd had more than enough of that!

'See you in a bit, Mum,' I said as I ran through the kitchen and out the back door.

'Don't be long, dear,' Mum called after me. 'Your dad's washing his hands and I'm just about to serve up.'

'OK!' I called and sprinted along the road to the corner shop.

I was back with the milk in double-quick time and careered down our path and into the back garden. As I belted around the corner I ran headlong into someone.

'Oof! Sorry, Dad!' I said.

'You should watch where you're going,' said a deep voice, clamping a pair of large hands on my shoulders.

'Whoa! Who are you?' I cried, trying to shake

myself free, but the man gripped me tight. 'Get off. Who are you?' I yelled, and stared angrily up at the stranger, seeing his face for the first time. The blood froze in my veins!

'Got you!' the man snarled.

Nabbed!

'Let me *mmmm*!' I began to shout, but my assailant clamped a hand over my mouth.

'I told you I'd track you to the ends of the earth, Charlie Small, and I always keep my promises!' he growled. 'I said I would see you hang and that's just what I intend to do. You're coming back with me, lad!'

I couldn't believe it – it was Joseph Craik, the deadliest enemy I'd made on my adventures! He was a thief-taker, a robber, a swindler and a no-good snivelling wretch also known as the Shadow. What the heck was he doing here?

'Where are you taking me?' I cried, struggling with all my might.

'To where you belong, Charlie,' Craik grinned as I looked desperately towards the house, hoping Mum or Dad would rush out to rescue me, but the house was silent and not even a curtain twitched.

'Let me go, you creep!' I bellowed.

'Never! You're going to pay for all the trouble you caused me,' sneered my old enemy as he pushed me back onto the street. I stared round in horror at the people and cars around me; everything had stopped moving as if frozen in time. It was like being in a film stuck on pause.

Oh, jeepers creepers! This is terrible; I have only just got home and now this ruffian is kidnapping me. Help me, someone, HELP!

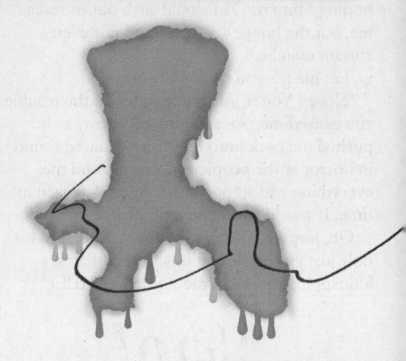

Where
is Craik
taking
Me?

charlie
Small
was here!

My worst enemies since starting on my adventures are (so far):

① The Puppet Master

② Joseph Craik — he never gives up!

③ Potentate of Mayazapan

④ The Giant Rats!

⑤ Thrak / Horatio Ham

⑥ Captain Cut-throat

Watch out, there's a giant rat behind you!

I've got to get away from Craik!
Got you at last!
uhoh!
Where are the badgers when you need them?
Aaaargh!

I wonder where
Knee-high is now.

I shall miss the
little peeping fellow!

This is
NOT
the end!

And that's
a promise,
charlie small